On the walk b
harbour Constan
**his own thoughts, giving Lisa all
the space she needed to scroll
through the events of an incredible
day.**

Lisa's lips were still burning from his kiss, and
how was she supposed to forget how aroused
that had made her? What might have happened
if he hadn't drawn back? Would she have lost
control? Just thinking about all the possibilities
was enough to excite her—

'I'll leave you now—'

Lisa's cheeks reddened guiltily as Tino
reclaimed her attention.

She smiled, remembering the moment Tino had
almost crashed into the harbour wall. He hadn't
come out of the day unscathed either. They had
both been equally distracted. Tossing her
battered sun hat on the bed, she freed her hair
and ran her fingers through the tangles. She
would take a long, lazy bath, and forget about
dangerous Greek men—she had to focus on
business now...

VIRGIN FOR SALE

BY
SUSAN STEPHENS

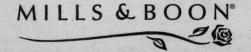

MILLS & BOON®

For Penny... a true friend.

First published in Great Britain 2005
Harlequin Mills & Boon Limited,
Eton House, 18-24 Paradise Road, Richmond, Surrey TW9 1SR

© Susan Stephens 2005

ISBN 0 263 84202 9

Set in Times Roman 10½ on 11½ pt.
01-1205-52329

Printed and bound in Spain
by Litografia Rosés, S.A., Barcelona

PROLOGUE

'YOU must leave before they come for you—'

Her mother's hands were biting into her shoulders making Lisa cry; silent tears that trickled down her cheeks unchecked, while her gaze remained locked on her mother's face.

'You must go to your father in the city.'

'My father?' Lisa's face turned suddenly fearful.

This was all the more shocking for her mother to see, because the child she called Willow had long ago learned to govern her feelings.

Lisa regained control quickly. She hated letting the mask slip. She only felt safe when no one knew what she was thinking. The mask was the shield she used to protect herself in the dangerous society in which she lived—a place where a careless glance or reckless laughter could lead to humiliating punishment in front of the whole community.

But if she was frightened of her ruthless 'family', Lisa was even more terrified of leaving her mother to their mercy. She was terrified of her father too, because he was a stranger her mother had fled from seven years before. Was her father wicked? Was that why her mother had run away? Was he even more wicked than the people who lived here?

Lisa stared fearfully at the open door. No one was allowed to close doors in the commune, let alone lock them.

'Please, Willow, please, you must go now, or they will be here.'

Her mother's voice had the desperate, pleading sound Lisa associated with horrible things, and her once beautiful eyes were bloodshot and watery. Her lips, tinged blue from the latest blows, were twisted in a grimace of desperation.

'Please, Willow—'

'Don't call me Willow. My name is Lisa...Lisa Bond.'

Hearing her mother's sob, Lisa wished she hadn't been the cause of it, and that she knew how to make her smile again. But she could only stand behind the barricades she had built in her mind, and watch her cry.

'I kept back some money from the market stall.'

Lisa looked on in horror as her mother dug inside the pocket of her flowing robe. 'But that's stealing from the community. You will be punished—'

'If you love me, you will take this and leave here.'

The coins hurt as they bit into the soft flesh of Lisa's palm. 'You'll come with me—'

'Come with you?'

For a moment, her mother's eyes brightened, but then they both heard the voices coming closer...men's voices.

'Climb through that window,' Eloisa instructed. Her voice was fierce and determined for the first, for the only time in her life. 'And don't stop running until you reach the bus depot. Here, take your father's address.' She pressed a slip of paper into Lisa's hand.

'But what about you?'

'I'll...I'll keep them here until you're far away.'

They exchanged a glance. There was no time for more. The leader of the commune had announced Lisa's initiation into womanhood that night at supper. It was an entertainment for everyone to enjoy, he said.

'My name is Lisa Bond. My name is Lisa Bond. My name is Lisa Bond.' Lisa chanted to herself as she hurtled down the pitch-black country lane. It was the only way she could block out the inner voice begging her to return to the commune and save her mother. Another, more rational voice insisted that if she did go back she would only cause her mother more pain.

When the lights of the small, local bus depot came into sight she sprinted the final few yards and launched herself onto the running board of the last bus to the city. There was no transport at the commune. She knew they couldn't get to her. At last, she was safe...

The man on board the bus took her money without comment. If he wondered at the grubby child clutching a slip of paper in a fist turned white with tension, something about the set of her mouth warned him not to intrude on her silence.

As Lisa gazed out into the darkness she was sure she could feel her mother's will urging her to turn her face to the future. And in that moment she knew for certain that somewhere deep inside her a person called Lisa Bond still existed. She would find that person, and nurture her like the seedlings she cared for in her own secret plot back at the wasteland the community called a garden. She had guarded them fiercely and controlled the weeds. In secure surroundings her plants had thrived, and so would she.

CHAPTER ONE

'SHE'S here—'

Constantine Zagorakis didn't move a muscle in response to his aide's whispered aside, though his eyes darkened a little as Lisa Bond entered the room. The woman's rise to the seat of power at Bond Steel had played right into his hands. Her late father, Jack Bond, had been a difficult character; doing business with Jack's daughter promised an easier ride.

Lisa Bond had a reputation in the City for being hard. In fairness she'd had to be hard-hearted to fill the shoes of her father when he'd died. But, hard or not, she was still a woman…and women were prey to their emotions, a factor that would give him an immediate advantage.

An air of confident command hung about the chairwoman of Bond Steel as she led her directors into the boardroom. Her manner challenged him. Lisa Bond wouldn't just dance to his tune; by the time he had finished with her, she'd sing to it too.

She'd had the worst kind of childhood, but his youth had been blighted too and he'd come through. He'd make no allowances. There were only two women in the world he could trust, and Lisa Bond was neither one of them.

Bond was a woman with history. Before throwing in her lot with her father, she had lived with her mother in a place that knew no rules or boundaries. She could turn on the ice all she liked, he wasn't buying it. Beneath that front there had to be a free spirit itching to break out. He would set that spirit free *and* add her company to his portfolio at a knock-down price. Where business was concerned he had no scruples. Breaking down the opposition was Constantine's primary objective.

Like any predator, Tino sensed the change in the air as Lisa Bond walked towards him, as well as the hint of some fresh scent she wore. She was dwarfed by the men in suits flanking her, but her presence more than made up for it. Petite and trim, she had clearly chosen her dark tailored suit to create a certain impression.

She was more beautiful than her photograph suggested, with luxuriant chestnut-brown hair fixed in an immaculate chignon. Beautiful women frequently used their looks like a weapon in an attempt to disarm him, but Lisa Bond was different—and not just because she had the most compelling sea-green eyes he had ever seen. She had something more. The outcome would be the same. He would take what he wanted and walk away. A woman had betrayed him at birth; only two had won his trust since then; there would be no more.

The tabloids and the business reports all said Bond was blessed with the attributes of an alpha male mixed together with the subtle cunning of a woman. The tempting sight of her breasts leant some credence to the rumour. Had she forgotten to fasten the extra button? Or was the curve of lush breasts exposed just enough to tease another cold calculation? Either way, it was his ineluctable duty to bring her to heel.

Tino took no more than a second or two over his assessment. His senses were tuned to the highest level. Whatever happened in the meeting, he would find the key that unlocked Bond Steel's darkest secrets. Every company had them. He and his people would simply sift through the records until he found out what they were. This 'negotiation' was merely a business courtesy—a gesture that meant nothing. The moment Bond Steel's Achilles heel was uncovered he would strike.

In the role of gracious victor he might save Ms Bond's backside—he might not. That would depend on how co-operative she was. The only certainty was that he would be adding another valuable asset to Zagorakis International Inc.

While this was going on, Lisa was drawing a few fast conclusions of her own, though it was hard to think rationally when her back was still bristling at the unannounced arrival of Constantine Zagorakis. Her diary was planned with all the care of a military operation; she didn't like it upset. The meeting with Zagorakis Inc had been scheduled for later that morning. She had something to sell; Zagorakis Inc was always hungry. But no one had expected Constantine Zagorakis to turn up in person.

Lisa had barely had chance to sit down at her desk before her PA, Mike, had alerted her to who was in the building... Zagorakis might as well have swept through it like a firestorm. Grown men were behaving like overexcited children at the mere mention of his presence. Fortunately, Lisa's speciality was dousing fires.

Zagorakis Inc had made an offer for one of Bond Steel's subsidiaries, a small engineering works that had done some good things in the past. The company no longer fitted her strategic vision for the core business, and the cash injection resulting from the sale could save Bond Steel.

Family-run businesses had dropped out of favour in the City, and the Bond Steel share price had taken a dive. The situation was critical. There were no other serious offers, and if she didn't nail the deal with Zagorakis she stood to lose Bond Steel, ruin the lives of those who worked for her, and face the type of humiliation that would put back the cause of women in industry a hundred years. Everything was riding on this deal.

Zagorakis Inc was cash rich and could move fast, which suited her perfectly. But that didn't explain why

Constantine Zagorakis was taking a personal interest in the deal. It was peanuts on the scale of his usual acquisitions. So, why was a world-class predator sniffing around? *Because he wanted all of Bond Steel?* That was where her suspicion dial was pointing.

When she found him staring at her, the rumour she had heard about him sprang to mind—he liked to look his prey in the eyes before devouring them. She'd laughed at the time—but now it didn't seem so funny.

She resented the Zagorakis-effect. He was like some vast power source that drew everyone's attention. A typical tycoon—he was ruthless, driven, and utterly heartless. She was no marshmallow herself, which explained the buzz in the building. This was one battle no one wanted to miss.

Some sixth sense had told him she never sat at the head of the table, but in the middle of her team. Unerringly, he had chosen to stand behind her chair as if he was already poised to take her place. And then he directed one of his minions to the seldom-used chairman's seat at the head of the table. *Who the hell did he think he was? Who was in control here?*

'Good morning, gentlemen.' She didn't need to raise her voice to command attention, though there was one dark gaze she could have done without. Zagorakis threw off sexual vibes with every move. And with treachery typical of the female body she was already longing for a slice of that high-octane maleness—something she had to get over fast.

Fortunately, she found that easy. She was Jack Bond's daughter, after all.

A bitter smile grazed Lisa's lips. Thanks to her father she had seen the depths of degradation to which a man could bring a woman. She had no intention of suffering her mother's fate, of being tossed around like some uncared for rag doll... She had to be in control.

Tino was immediately aware of the shadow dulling

Lisa's gaze. He had been anticipating a glint of challenge, or some proof of her wild nature. This new, subdued expression was a real disappointment. The hunt was spoiled before it began if the prey was wounded.

He was relieved when she quickly recovered. His imagination was in overdrive. She had probably missed an appointment at the beauty salon.

Lisa consciously relaxed her shoulder. It was dangerous to let Zagorakis see how shaken she was, but something about him reminded her of the past…

It was his presence, his strength—his overwhelming physical strength. Yes, that was it. She shook her head in a fast, instinctive gesture to close the door on those memories that were safer locked away. But for a few seconds the old film replayed in her head. The leader of the commune had been a powerful, awe-inspiring figure, but he had been an evil man, who had grown ever stronger by feeding on the insecurities of his flock.

It had been Lisa's misfortune to come to his notice when her body had started developing faster than the other girls', and she would always be grateful to her mother for helping her to run away before the obscene initiation ceremony he had planned especially for her could take place.

She glanced around quickly just to check that no one had noticed her brush with the past. No one had. They were all too busy preparing for the meeting. And now the blood was flowing freely through her veins again, and she could feel her cheeks warming up. The past would always be with her, Lisa reflected grimly. And thank goodness for it, it kept her wary, kept her safe.

'Ms Bond.'

She came to abruptly. Zagorakis was offering to shake her hand in greeting, yet all she could think was how threatening he was. She thought about her father, remembering how his icy control had proved too much for his much younger wife, causing her mother to bolt from the endless round of coffee mornings and race days to the promised freedom of the commune. Her father might have been the mainstay of every charitable committee in the area, but he had remained blind to the fact that her mother's fragile psyche had been falling to pieces in front of him...

'I'm going to be a free spirit,' her mother had said, Lisa recalled, curling her lip as she remembered their hectic flight to the commune. The only thing that was free at the commune as far as she remembered was the men's licence to have sex whenever, and with whomever, they chose. The women worked, while the men drank themselves into oblivion, only recovering in time for the next rut.

In Lisa's opinion, her mother had simply exchanged one type of savage slavery for another. Fortunately, such a thing could never happen to her. She had taken control of her life when she had escaped the commune, and no one would ever take that control away from her. If they did she always feared it would destroy her.

As Constantine Zagorakis's hand enclosed Lisa's in the customary handshake she felt a shock run right up her arm. She had thought him strong, but she'd had no idea up to that moment how powerful he was. Touching him was like touching the pelt of a sleeping lion. She could sense the power underneath. And he had the same peculiar stillness of a deadly predator, a predator poised to pounce...

'It's a pleasure to meet you,' she said, but they both knew it was a meaningless courtesy; the smile didn't even attempt to reach her eyes. The only pleasure in store for either of them was a deal that came out weighted in their favour.

Zagorakis's gaze was as hard as her own. She wished it might have been possible to learn something about him before they had met, but Constantine Zagorakis was a dark mystery of a man, a man who lived his life behind a wall of secrecy. No rumours about him had ever circulated. He was, apparently, Mr Clean, with no family that anyone knew about, no lurid sex life, no life at all outside his formidable business empire—an empire that reached into every corner of the world.

At thirty-five, Constantine Zagorakis ran one of the largest corporations on the planet. Devouring companies was his recreation of choice. But this was one business that would stick in his craw, because Bond Steel wasn't for sale. And neither was she. Lisa thought, hardening her mouth when he held her gaze. Easing her hand away from his clasp, she turned to address the room: 'Shall we sit down, gentlemen?'

And now, Zagorakis was holding out her chair like the perfect gentleman. He didn't fool her. He understood the significance of the seat of power, and was goading her with it. He had sensed how territorial she was. The fact that he could read her so accurately made her doubly cautious. 'Thank you, Mr Zagorakis.' She took her place.

'Please, call me Tino.'

'Won't you sit across from me?' Lisa indicated a place at the table, ignoring his attempt at informality. She didn't want to sit facing him, but it was better, safer to keep him in sight at all times—that way she could detect any little asides he might send to his people.

It provided her with a perfect chance to study him. His choice of outfit was nothing short of an insult: casual jacket, blue jeans, and a black, open-necked shirt—though everything was designer, she'd give him that. Still, he looked more like a buccaneer home from a raid than a suave Greek tycoon. His thick, wavy black hair was too long, and there was at least a day's worth of stubble on his face.

Her stomach gave a kick as their eyes briefly met. She didn't like his expression. Aesthetically his eyes were pleasing enough, glorious in fact, black as pitch, with lashes so long he could almost shield what he was thinking...but not quite. This was a scouting trip for Tino Zagorakis. He wasn't interested in her small engineering works. He was testing the vulnerability of the parent company, Bond Steel. He was testing *her* vulnerability.

Lisa was used to corporate raiders sniffing around. They all thought the same thing: a woman at the helm was easy pickings—their mistake. Zagorakis was no more of a threat than the rest—other than in the hot-sexual-tug department.

Businessmen she normally encountered had boardroom pallor with blubber to match, and so she had imagined him shorter, dumpier, uglier—a younger model of the grizzled old shipping tycoons. Tino Zagorakis was none of those things.

But she had to forget the man's impressive casing, and focus on the brain beneath. Bond Steel's reputation was on the firing line—not to mention her own, and from his casual approach she assumed Zagorakis thought the deal a foregone conclusion. He hadn't even troubled to shave or dress appropriately, and that showed contempt in her book.

The meeting between Bond Steel and Zagorakis Inc evolved like a polite game of tennis, with the tactical ball being passed with exaggerated politeness between the two sides. Meanwhile, Lisa concentrated her mind on the subtext: Zagorakis had identified a company he thought a good match with his own; the small portion she was prepared to sell didn't interest him; he wanted it all.

When a lull came in their discussions, he stood up. It was barely noon. 'Are you leaving so soon? I've arranged for a buffet to be laid out next door. I thought we could discuss some of the finer details.' He wasn't interested in making small talk over canapés—and it was time to lose the charm. 'We haven't finished, Mr Zagorakis—'

'I have.'

Lisa felt the blood drain out of her face. She wasn't used

to being looked at the way Zagorakis was looking at her. She wasn't used to anyone going against her wishes. She made the rules; everyone else lived by them—that way they all stayed safe. But Tino Zagorakis had made it clear that as far as he was concerned she had no rank. He would do exactly as *he* pleased, and she could go hang. Bond Steel was just a tasty snack...the company, the people who worked there, counted for nothing.

'I regret I have another appointment.' He held her gaze.

Regret? Lisa didn't think so. That deep, husky voice was pitched to make it sound as if there were some type of understanding between them, an intimacy almost. It unsettled her, and must have unsettled her team—they had to be wondering what was going on. Without raising his voice Zagorakis had scored a telling point by subtly undermining her authority. And then she saw that his eyes were hard and calculating, and even slightly mockingly amused.

Scraping back her chair, she stood to face him. She wasn't about to let Bond Steel be gobbled down by some ravenous tycoon—a tycoon who thought her company was just a set of numbers. Bond Steel wasn't a counter to be risked. And if Zagorakis had come down from his ivory tower to measure her, and judged her no threat, he had miscalculated. She would defend Bond Steel to the last.

After her experience in the commune Bond Steel had been her salvation. While other teenagers had longed for freedom, she had craved discipline and boundaries so she could sleep safe at night. Jack Bond had given her that. Before she'd started to work for him he had sent her to a school where even the rigid order had been welcome. It had provided her with a framework within which she had felt safe, and she had excelled. When she had returned home she hadn't cared that her father had shown her no favouritism; she had never expected any. Jack Bond had only ever wanted a son, and she accepted that too. She had worked her way up her father's company from the bottom. When he'd died, she'd taken his place thanks to sheer dint of effort. By then she had discovered the key to his success. It was nothing more than hard work and focus. Jack Bond had never allowed anything as time-wasting as emotion to stand in his way.

'Why, Ms Bond, you seem distracted.'

Those eyes—those incredible black-gold eyes—were dancing with laughter. Sucking in an angry gulp of air, Lisa felt her hands ball into fists. 'Not a bit of it, Mr Zagorakis.' Her gaze flicked over him dismissively. 'As your decision to attend this meeting was clearly last-minute, I won't keep you. I'm sure our people can arrange another time for us to meet if there are any outstanding details—'

'Shall we say dinner at nine to discuss those outstanding details?'

Lisa's cheeks flamed red. She was sure the *double entendre* was intended. In spite of her slender frame her breasts had always been regarded as her most 'outstanding' feature. And now her nipples had hardened into bullets, which, from the expression in Zagorakis's eyes, she guessed he knew.

'I'll have my chauffeur pick you up around nine at your apartment—'

'No—' Before she could say more Lisa found herself staring at an open door. 'Gentlemen, this meeting is over,' she said, quickly recovering her self-possession. 'Tomorrow morning at ten would suit me for the follow up. Arrange it for me, will you, Mike?'

By nine o' clock that evening Lisa was curled up tensely on the sofa at the penthouse she called home. Warm and pink after her bath, she was anything but relaxed. Wearing her favourite plush robe, she had the music turned down low, a crystal goblet of good burgundy on the side table next to her, and a new book just started. She had read the first page three times, and still didn't have a clue what it said.

Zagorakis's chauffeur would call round, she knew that, but still she flinched and dragged her robe a little closer when the doorbell rang. Thankfully Vera would take care of it. Vera, confidante and housekeeper, knew exactly what she had to do.

Just as Lisa had anticipated, the exchange between Vera and Zagorakis's chauffeur lasted no more than a few seconds. With a sigh of relief, she turned back to her book. But she couldn't relax… She tried changing the music. She could always find something to suit her mood amongst her vast collection of CD's… Tonight was different, tonight she had to force her fingers past the boxed sets devoted to the heavenly voice of *La Divina* Callas. The impassioned Greek-American voice of Maria Anna Sophie Cecilia Kalogeropoulos was the last thing she needed to hear. Right now anything remotely Greek was off limits. Finally, she settled for some low, smoochy jazz. The plangent wail of Miles Davis' trumpet seemed appropriate somehow.

Returning to her book, Lisa turned the pages dutifully, all the time trying to ignore the keen dark eyes and mocking smile occupying her thoughts. When the doorbell rang again she was surprised and then angry. Zagorakis had some nerve sending his chauffeur round twice in one evening. Couldn't he take a hint?

Vera answered the door, but Lisa's curiosity got the better of her. Padding barefoot across the room, she froze. The man's audacity was unbelievable. His unannounced visit to her office building had been bad enough, but this was outrageous—and Vera was having trouble getting rid of him.

'Thank you, Vera, I'll see to this.'

Lisa couldn't pretend she wasn't thankful that Vera remained hovering in the background. 'Yes?' She stared up at him. Tino Zagorakis was more casually dressed, and even more brazenly male. Without a jacket she could see how toned he was beneath his black shirt. His assessing stare was every bit as hard as she remembered.

'We arranged to have dinner tonight.'

'*You* arranged to have dinner tonight, *Mr* Zagorakis.'

'It's time you called me Tino.'

Oh, really? 'It's late—'

'Exactly,' he said. 'And as you pointed out, *Lisa*, we still have things to talk about.'

Lisa? When did she give him permission to use her first name? Jack Bond's first law of survival: keep everyone at a distance. *Everyone…* She relaxed minutely. He was carrying a briefcase. Of course, Zagorakis was a man who would far rather trade than indulge his carnal appetites, but she had already set up their next meeting for the following morning. She had no intention of being railroaded by him twice in one day. 'Business will have to wait until our respective teams are present.'

'If you insist.'

'I do insist. Our next meeting will be held tomorrow morning.'

'Thank you for reminding me…but we still have to eat.'

His casual shrug and the smile that accompanied it threw her, and while she was trying to figure out his angle he walked past her into the apartment.

'Like I said, *Mr* Zagorakis—' she went after him '—it's late—'

'And so I took the trouble of ordering in.' He paused mid-step to turn round and look at her. 'I didn't want to put your housekeeper to any trouble.'

And now Vera was sharing a flirtatious smile with him! What was this? A conspiracy?

In fairness, she couldn't blame Vera; the man was hot. His shirt was open far enough to show some hard, tanned chest, and his blue jeans appeared pressure-moulded to thighs of iron. And there were certain other impressive bulges below the heavy-duty belt…

'Are you sure you don't mind me coming inside?'

Lisa quickly adjusted her gaze. The only thing sure about this was that her face was heating up. 'I don't wish to appear ungrateful.'

'But?' he pressed.

'I'm tired. It's late. And I'm ready for bed.'

'So I see.'

His lips tugged up at one corner in a way that made her painfully aware that she was naked beneath her robe. The split second it took to look down to check that the robe was securely fastened was enough for his chauffeur to march past her carrying a hamper. 'Where do you think you're going?'

Zagorakis stepped forward and barred her way. 'In here?' he said, protecting his man's back by resting one arm against the doorframe of her den.

Lisa's mouth dropped open. The only thing left for her to confirm, apparently, was the venue for the picnic he had brought with him. 'You have some incredible nerve—'

'Please…no more compliments.' He held up his hands in mock defeat and she had to be prodded twice before Vera could make her presence felt.

'Hadn't you better get changed?' Vera suggested discreetly. 'You don't want him guessing you're naked under there.'

Lisa could see the sense in that. 'Stay with them, will you, Vera? I'll be back as quickly as I can.'

Jeans and a T-shirt might have been a practical choice, but smart navy trousers and a tailored white blouse made Lisa feel more in control. The sex-stripping pop socks and boring flat shoes were an inspiration, and, with her hair scraped back into a pony-tail, she was satisfied that she had done everything possible to strip anything lightweight from her appearance. A slick of clear lip-gloss was her only concession—but then she sucked it off again. No point in playing Zagorakis's game—she'd stick to her own.

The angry words she had been rehearsing all the way down from her bedroom died the moment she entered her den. The room had been transformed. Candles had been lit, and were flickering on every surface. Champagne was cooling in a bucket…and on a low table between the two sofas a platter of fresh seafood emitted a faint, salty tang. Another mouth-watering aroma said the bread in the wicker basket was still warm, and, inside a crystal bowl nestling in a dish of ice, yellow butter pats were asking to be slathered over one of the crisp, golden crusts. And she was hungry—starving, in fact, Lisa realised, praying her stomach wouldn't rumble.

'Can I tempt you?'

Transferring her gaze to Constantine Zagorakis's dark, slanting eyes, Lisa stared at him coldly.

'A few prawns, perhaps?' he murmured, reaching for a plate.

He was baiting his hook with a lot more than seafood, Lisa suspected, seeing the smile hovering around his mouth.

'What's the matter?' He put the plate down again.

Lisa had been distracted momentarily. She was sure she had just heard two sets of footsteps leaving the apartment; two voices mingling as the front door closed.

'Where are you going now?' he said.

Lisa looked down at the hand on her arm. Zagorakis released her at once. 'It's nothing,' she said. 'I must have been mistaken—'

'Mistaken?'

'I thought I heard Vera leaving.'

'Your housekeeper? You did.'

'No.' Lisa shook her head. 'Vera would have come to say goodnight to me before she left.'

'Not if she was being discreet.'

'Discreet?'

His shoulders eased in a shrug. 'It's no trouble for my chauffeur to take her home. He passes her door—'

Raising one hand, Lisa silenced him. 'Let me get this straight. *You* sent my housekeeper home?'

'It's getting late.'

'I would have called a taxi.'

'I thought I'd save you the trouble.'

'Trouble?' Trouble had come through her door at nine o' clock that morning and she hadn't got rid of him yet.

'That's all right with you, isn't it Lisa?'

Lisa? She wasn't going to let him get to her, even though he was asking one thing while his eyes were suggesting something else. She had no intention of giving him the satisfaction of seeing her shrink from the prospect of being alone with him either. 'Yes, *Tino*, that's absolutely fine with me—'

'Good.'

He seemed pleased to have got that out of the way, and then her guard must have dropped because he raised her hand to his lips and dropped a kiss on the back of it.

'I realise it's late.' He tried for contrite. 'Do you forgive me?'

Lisa snatched her hand away. 'Do you always march uninvited into other people's homes?'

His lips pressed down ruefully, *attractively*…

'I'm sorry, Lisa, I thought we had both earned some down-time.'

He was sorry? She didn't think so. But since when could someone brush a hand with his lips and set a whole body on fire?

'Don't you ever relax?' he pressed, his perceptive gaze refusing to release her.

'When I'm given the opportunity.'

'Surely you must get out of this starchy uniform of yours, and kick back once in a while?'

'Surprisingly, I tried to do that very thing this evening. I took a long, warm bath, slipped into a comfy robe, and came down here…to relax.'

Touché,' he murmured softly.

Lisa sighed with frustration. Technically, Zagorakis was her guest—and she couldn't forget that his money could rescue her company. She couldn't afford to be too rude to him—and the food did look delicious…

'Why don't you let me choose something for you?' he suggested, picking up the plate again.

'I can manage, thank you. Really, you don't need to—' Raising her voice, she was forced to insist, 'Give me that plate.'

'Certainly.'

By the time she went to take it from him it was loaded with delicacies—but he kept his grip on it, so that she was bound to him by a too-small china plate…and when he stubbornly resisted her attempt to pull it free she could feel her cheeks start to burn. 'You really didn't need to go to all this trouble.' She tugged a little harder, refusing to give him the upper hand.

'It was my pleasure, I assure you.'

'Why exactly?'

'Perhaps you deserve a little spoiling. Perhaps we both do.'

It was hardly the answer she had been anticipating—and certainly not when it was delivered in that frank and engaging way. His eyes were so deep she was in danger of drowning in them, and they were standing far too close. The warmth of his body was curling round her like a seductive cloak and she could almost forget that, as far as Bond Steel was concerned, Constantine Zagorakis was arch enemy number one—

Breaking eye contact, she pulled away.

'Champagne?' he said pleasantly.

She was still fighting off his powerful sexual aura. But then common sense kicked in: definitely no champagne. She loved it, but she wanted to keep her wits about her. What she should do was go to the kitchen, fill a jug with iced water, and pour it over both of them. 'Thank you, I'd love a glass of champagne.'

The expression in his eyes should have brought her to her senses. She was on the point of crossing an invisible line, a line she knew she always had to stay behind. She only had to remember her mother's fate to know that she could lose everything, if she ever allowed her senses to take the lead…but she couldn't risk antagonising Tino Zagorakis. He was a formidable business opponent, and on a personal level perhaps even more dangerous…but fore-warned was forearmed—and one glass of champagne couldn't hurt.

As Tino handed her the glass of champagne he lifted his own and tipped it towards her in a silent toast. She replied by walking away to perch on the edge of the room's only straight-backed chair. She needed a moment to collect her-self. This encounter was something new for her. In the past men had always been happy to follow her lead, which was hardly surprising since most of her relationships were con-ducted in her head—she didn't have time or inclination for anything else. She liked her life the way it was—tidy, suc-cessful, and absolutely safe.

'Are you sure you're comfortable over there?'

In spite of all her good intentions, the look Tino gave her made Lisa's heart pound. If nothing else Tino Zagorakis set new standards for her fantasies. 'I'm fine, thank you.'

'More champagne?'

'Why not?' She could handle it. She could handle him too.

As he crossed the room she noticed that his movements were fluid like the big cat she had first thought him. Moving on silent feet, he reached her side before she even had time to hold out her glass.

He left her alone after that, and they ate in silence seated at opposite ends of the room, which should have been a relief. But Lisa's sensory self had taken over from the rational side of her being. The delicious food and wine slithered down her throat with dizzying speed, and the alcohol loosened her inhibitions. Some very primitive thoughts were entering her mind...just watching his mouth work as he ate was compulsive viewing; his teeth were so white and strong, his lips so firm, and mobile—

'Lisa?' He picked up on her stare. 'Would you like something more?'

As Lisa's eyes cleared she waved the bread basket away and she shook her head. 'No, thank you...that was absolutely delicious, but I couldn't eat another thing.'

'Then I think it's time we got to know each other a little better, don't you?'

CHAPTER TWO

TINO took her plate, stacking it with his on a side table. Lisa watched warily as he came towards her, and almost flinched when he was close enough to touch. But then, instead of grabbing her, he snatched hold of his briefcase and dipped inside. Bringing out some financial reports, he spread them across the low table between them.

'I think we both know you've got a few problems, Lisa—'

For a moment when his glance flicked up Lisa thought he was talking about something other than business, and blushed violently.

'I've noticed a few discrepancies here and there,' he continued. 'All easily explained, I'm sure. No doubt our respective bean-counters will soon iron things out.'

It was a relief for her mind to click back into business mode.

'Take a look at these.' He passed her some sheets. 'It's only fair that you should have sight of all my findings.'

Fair? Tino was pointing up the fact that he had uncovered a whole clutch of Bond Steel skeletons in the shortest time imaginable, in order to prepare her for a much reduced offer price, Lisa suspected. 'That's very good of you, Tino.'

She was careful to sound noncommittal. She wanted to see exactly what he had found out before showing any reaction to it.

'I'll leave the rest of these for you.' He closed his briefcase.

'You're going?'

'Not if you don't want me to.'

He had changed in a heartbeat from cold-blooded businessman to someone very different. Her pulse rate quickened in response. But this was wrong. Worse than wrong, it was dangerous.

Her gaze was drawn to his hand resting on the door…his strong, supple hand resting on the door. 'I'll see you out.' Her voice sounded distant and undecided. It was as if she were looking down at herself, or rather at the woman she might have been if her life had been different. She didn't want him to leave. The apartment would be so empty without him… She would be lonely again. Lonely but safe.

Tino had tossed a pebble into the pond and waited to see how far the ripples would travel. He had to admit he was surprised. She had capitulated rather sooner than he had imagined. Mixing business and pleasure was new to him, but for Lisa he would make an exception. He wanted Bond Steel, and he wanted Lisa Bond. Business was a game he always won, and she had become part of that game.

She thought herself strong and controlling. How strong? How controlling? He would test her boundaries and find out. His body ached for release. The thought of dominating Lisa held real appeal. It would be to her benefit too, of course. If she had the good sense to surrender he would give her the ride of her life.

As Tino caught hold of her arm Lisa snapped out of the trance. 'That's the second time you've done that,' she told him angrily, 'and I don't like it.'

'Really? Then you must forgive me,' he said in a voice that managed to be both penitent and amused.

But he didn't let her go.

And now they were close, too close, and their breath was mingling. There was no sound other than the two of them breathing. And then, perhaps by accident, the joint of his thumb brushed the side of her breast, and she sighed.

He felt her tense as he accidentally touched her when he shifted position, but that sigh was sending out a very different message. She didn't try to pull away, and now he felt the tremor running through her. He could feel it coursing right up his arm.

She wasn't jaded, and that pleased him. Her experience in the commune had only prepared her for him, heightened her capacity for pleasure... He allowed his gaze to slip to her breasts, to the full swell pressing urgently against her chaste white business shirt. He centred his attention on the taut nipples straining against the lace of her bra, and was gratified to see them harden still more beneath his interest. Lifting his head, he saw the pulse fluttering in her neck and the pink flush of desire tinting her skin. He understood her torment. He understood it and therefore would prolong it.

He was rewarded when the tip of her tongue crept out to moisten her lips. She fully expected him to kiss her. But instead he stared into her eyes, gauging her level of arousal. As he had anticipated they were almost black with desire, with just a faint rim of green remaining. She was breathing fast and the tiny gasps were making the fabric pull against the buttons on the front of her shirt. He longed to rip it off—but he wouldn't do that, because he knew she would like it too much.

She was quivering with frustration. She had never been so aroused. *She had never been aroused by a man before...* She could control most things, *all* things—so why not this? And why wouldn't he kiss her? One kiss was all she wanted, and then she would kick him out. She licked her lips, and saw his attention drawn to the full swell of her bottom lip.

Her lips were moist where she had touched them with her tongue...swollen with desire. He recognised all the signs, and, though he planned it to be this way, the sight was nearly too much for him. Dragging her close, he held her so their lips were almost touching, raising the danger level for them both.

She responded, and white-hot passion flared between them, but at the very point when he intended to pull back and teach her a lesson she stiffened and made an angry sound low in her throat. She strained against him—not with passion now, but with absolute determination to break free. He released her at once.

'Get out.' Her voice was barely above a whisper, but it contained more venom than he had ever heard. She didn't look at him. She remained frozen in place, with the back of her hand covering her mouth as if she wanted to hide it from him, wanted to hide the signs of her arousal from him. And she had been aroused, but then so had he.

'Get out,' she repeated, snapping the words at him.

In place of his surprise, Tino felt his anger beginning to rise. 'Why?' he said. 'Because I almost kissed you before you could kiss me?'

'Is that what you think?' She looked at him incredulously.

His pride was all over the place. He had never misjudged a situation so badly. 'Don't tell me you didn't want that?'

She rallied then, straightening up to confront him, her face drained of colour. 'You'll be telling me I deserved it next.'

'What? You think passion between a man and a woman is some form of punishment?' He grasped the back of his neck with his hand, and the look on his face told Lisa she was wrong about him—horribly wrong.

Straightening up, he stared at her coldly. 'I don't need these mind games, Lisa.'

'Then get out!' She made an angry gesture. 'What are you waiting for?'

'When are you going to learn that not everyone wants to dance to your tune?'

'Or yours?' Her eyes were blazing. She thought she heard him murmur something more. 'What did you say?'

'I said, you're nothing but a control freak, Lisa.' He stared straight at her so there could be no mistake.

Lisa didn't show by even a flicker that he had come closer than any man alive to proving that a lie. 'I think you'd better leave now.'

'That's the first thing you've said this evening that makes any sense.'

'What do you mean, she didn't make the meeting?'

Shifting the satellite phone to his other shoulder, Tino stared out at the clouds above Stellamaris, his private island, barely seeing the beloved contours of lush greenery, sugar sand and rock as he listened to what his right hand man was trying to tell him.

'They said she was sick—'

'Sick?'

'I don't know, Tino. I couldn't find out any more. I don't think it's serious, headache perhaps, women's problems— who the hell knows?'

'Find out for me, will you? And get back to me right away.'

'I'll do the best I can.'

Tino's voice hardened. 'That's not good enough, Andreas.'

'OK, leave it with me.'

'And, Andreas...'

'Yes?'

'Start making overtures to Clifton Steel, will you?'

'Clifton? But I thought you wanted Bond—'

Tino's voice was uncompromising. 'Just do as I ask, Andreas.'

'Yes, boss.'

He couldn't afford to feel like this about anyone, let alone Lisa Bond. Have her occupy his thoughts to the exclusion of everything else? Was he mad? After what had happened between them, professionally, he'd bury her. He would buy out Clifton *and* Bond. That would solve the problem—permanently. By the time he had finished with her she would never want to hear his name again.

Cutting the connection, Tino eased back in the leather armchair he used when he wasn't flying the jet himself. His eyes narrowed as he thought over the events of the past forty-eight hours. He had never met anyone like Lisa Bond. She had blind-sided him, slipped beneath his control. She had led him on, and then pulled back at the last moment.

But she was a woman in her late twenties, and grown women didn't behave that way. The signals they gave off were always clear. Why were Lisa's signals so misleading? Her behaviour puzzled him, and he didn't like puzzles. She was acting like a kid, a virgin, even, rather than the ball-breaking bitch everyone said she was.

And why was he still thinking about her at all? Had Lisa Bond turned his shrew-capping tactic on its head, and squirrelled her way into his limited bank of caring instincts? He had always imagined those instincts had been beaten out of him in his youth, but she had made him look at her as more than a business adversary.

He couldn't afford to go soft. With a gust of exasperation, Tino released his seat belt before the jet touched down. He was impatient to breathe the fresh clean air of Stellamaris. When Lisa Bond came back into his life he would be ready for her. And she would come back, they all did. She wanted the same thing everyone else did—his money. It always came down to that in the end.

*   *   *

'What do you mean, he didn't turn up?' Lisa demanded, rolling over onto her stomach in bed so that she could rest her chin on her hand.

'Just that,' Mike, her PA, assured her. 'Everyone else was here, of course—just you two were missing.'

'Don't bracket me with that man. I have no idea where Constantine Zagorakis is, but, I can assure you, he's not here with me. Make certain everyone else knows that too, will you, Mike?'

'So, what's up? You never take time off.'

That was true. Like her father, only a stretcher carting her off to hospital could get in the way of her work. Mike knew that as well as she did. But her one-to-one with Tino had left Lisa more shaken than she had expected.

'Lisa, what's happened?'

She refocused. 'Don't worry, Mike. I have a sore throat, that's all.'

'A sore throat?' He sounded unconvinced. 'I'm sorry.'

Lisa had known Mike since they were at school together. She hated lying to him. He had already brought her up to speed with what she'd missed at the meeting, and yet she felt he was holding something back. 'So, what's the gossip on the street?'

'It's more than gossip. But there's good news as well as bad.'

'Just give me the bad.' She steeled herself.

'I got a call.'

All the humour had just leached from Mike's voice, Lisa realised. 'Go on,' she pressed grimly.

'From my pal at Clifton.'

'Clifton Steel?' Mike's silence confirmed it. 'And?'

'Zagorakis Inc have asked for an initial meeting with Clifton. Apparently they're considering—'

'Their small engineering plant?' Lisa's stomach clenched with dread as she cut across him.

'No, Lisa, the whole of Clifton—'

She went cold. 'But they can't—' This time Zagorakis had really caught her out. How could anyone move that fast? 'But what about our deal with Zagorakis Inc?'

'Word is Zagorakis has gone cold on our small works. It's all or nothing for him. I heard in the last hour that he's asked his people to start courting Clifton…and, Lisa…'

'Yes?' Lisa tensed, wondering what else there could be.

'He's after us too—'

'No,' Lisa exploded, sitting bolt upright. It was everything she had been dreading. 'Bond Steel isn't for sale, Mike. I only need to sell the small works. The cash injection that will bring is all we need to set us back on our feet.'

'It may be too late.'

'We're not going to give up, and throw Bond Steel to the lions.'

'To one lion in particular, you mean?'

'Get Zagorakis on the phone.'

'Who do you want to speak to?'

'Tino, of course.'

'He doesn't speak to anyone directly.'

'He'll speak to me.'

'What if he won't?'

'Do anything you have to do to get his private number, Mike,' Lisa pressed grimly.

'It won't help you.'

'What do you mean it won't help me?

'He took off at dawn to fly to his private island in Greece. There's no way anyone can contact him there—even his staff aren't allowed to do that. They have to wait for Zagorakis to ring them.'

'But that's ridiculous.'

'Maybe. But that's the way it is.'

'Are you sure about this?'

'Totally. I've got a friend at Clifton.'

Lisa's mind raced. 'The financial director? That tall, good-looking blond guy?'

'We're seeing each other, Lisa.'

'I guessed.' A faint smile broke through Lisa's tension. 'I hope you'll both be very happy.' That explained how Mike had learned everything so fast, and also confirmed that everything he had told her was one-hundred-per-cent accurate. And without the cash from the sale of the small works to Zagorakis Inc, she was in serious trouble.

'Shall I give you the good news now?'

'Good news? I can't believe you can have anything good to tell me after that.'

'You are fit to fly.'

'Anything but a joke.'

'This is no joke. The Bond Steel company jet has just been signed off. It's ready to go when you are.'

'Mike, that's not good news—or had you forgotten the purpose behind selling the engineering works? We can't stand more expense right now. If things get any worse than they are the jet will be the first thing that has to go.'

'Sell it by all means—but not yet, Lisa,' Mike insisted. 'Zagorakis's island is quite small. The landing strip can't take commercial airliners.'

Lisa's tense face softened abruptly. 'Mike, you're an angel! I need one clear day to prepare,' she added, thinking aloud. 'So, make sure the jet is fully fuelled and ready to fly on Sunday. Have the pilot file a flight plan for Stellamaris—'

'So, you're chasing Zagorakis?'

Mike was smart—that was why she had hired him in the first place. But after what he had told her, she was going to Stellamaris, not just to save the deal, but to nail Zagorakis to the mast. 'No, Mike,' she assured him, 'I'm chasing business.'

*   *   *

Stellamaris was beautiful. So beautiful, it made Lisa want to cry. And she never cried. Well, not since she was a child. Never in her adult life had she ever shed a tear—except on Friday morning after Mike's phone call. But those had been very different tears—Mike would have said she was having a tantrum and he would have been right. Everything within reach had been thrown at the wall. And then she had wasted another hour clearing up the mess. She never lost control. She never would again after that. What a time-wasting loss of energy that had been. *Sore throat?* Sore head was closer to the truth. Did Tino Zagorakis really think he could direct events that, not only affected her own life, but the lives of people she cared about, from his private island?

'We're nearly there, Thespinis Bond. When I turn the next corner, you will be able to see the villa.'

Then I'll close my eyes, Lisa thought, remembering to thank the kindly taxi driver. How was she going to look at Tino's ugly villa after feasting her eyes on a clear aquamarine ocean, ochre-tinted cliffs, and pale sugar sand? The fields they had passed had all been bathed in a mellow golden light, and there was a huge orange ball of a sun hanging low out to sea. She was sure Tino would live in some vast, overblown carbuncle, possibly with gold-plated walls, and certainly with a flagpole to show when he was in residence. Hideously opulent, and grotesquely vulgar, it was sure to be an eyesore after everything else she had seen on Stellamaris... Or not. 'Is this it?' she said with surprise, leaning forward in her seat.

'*Ne*, Thespinis Bond,' the taxi driver confirmed, 'this is Villa Aphrodite. Very beautiful, isn't she?'

'Yes, she is,' Lisa agreed without blinking. 'Very beautiful indeed.' Tino's villa was cloaked in white marble that shimmered peach and umber where the muted light washed over it, and even the shadows came in a tasteful shade of magenta. She imagined the walls might turn to a delicate shade of pink in the first rays of dawn... The building was large, but even without stepping inside Lisa guessed there would be rooms for formal entertaining as well as cosier rooms in which you could live in comfort all year round. The entrance would be grand and imposing, but beyond that there would be secret hideaways—a home within a palace, rather than a showpiece, as she had been dreading...*Tino's home*...

'I expect Constantine is down on the beach.'

The elderly taxi driver cut into her thoughts. The warmth and familiarity with which he spoke the name immediately rang alarm bells in Lisa's mind, reminding her that Zagorakis was a complex animal—and one she must be constantly wary of.

'Unfortunately you can't see the beach from up here.'

Half turning to her, the taxi driver reclaimed Lisa's attention, angling his shoulders while watching the road. 'Tino only arrived on Friday, so I expect he will be washing all the stresses of the city out of his mind.'

Stresses of the city? She'd give him stresses, Lisa mused grimly as her thoughts turned to her mission. If Constantine Zagorakis thought he could ditch their deal by remote control while he was enjoying a swim in the sea, he was sadly mistaken.

'It's the first thing he does when he comes home to Stellamaris,' the taxi driver continued, unaware of the tensions building in the seat behind him. 'Tino loves the ocean, like all Greeks...'

Lisa let his friendly chatter roll over her. It didn't seem possible the taxi driver was talking about the same man. Even the thought of that brute having something called a home seemed unlikely. Surely Tino Zagorakis lived out of suitcases, always restless, always searching out the next deal?

She sat back as the taxi pulled through some tall

wrought-iron gates, preparing herself with some deep steadying breaths. They were travelling slowly down a long, neatly groomed avenue lined with trees. Leading up to the grand villa, it dissected a garden bursting with flowers. In such a hot climate the irrigation alone would be a mammoth task.

'It is almost May Day—a significant day on Stellamaris. The gardens are at their best.'

Lisa met the taxi driver's gaze in the driver's mirror.

'Soon everyone will be gathering flowers to decorate their houses,' he went on. 'You are visiting Stellamaris at the most romantic time of year.'

Lisa's lips firmed. 'The villa seems to be built on top of a cliff,' she said, to distract him from a topic she had no interest in pursuing. 'How do you get down to the beach?'

'There are steps cut into the cliff face,' he explained, 'but Tino has had a funicular fitted to make it easier for his friend.'

'His friend?'

'His elderly friend.'

Constantine Zagorakis had more than one friend? That seemed unlikely.

'And here we are,' the taxi driver declared, halting at the foot of some impressive marble steps. Yanking on the handbrake, he switched off the engine.

In spite of everything she had planned—keeping a cool head, securing the deal at any price, etc—Lisa's heart was thundering. What was she doing here? What was she really doing here? She should have asked for Tino's e-mail address, and communicated with him safely on that level—impersonally.

Smoothing down her suit jacket, she paid the driver. It didn't help that she felt so hot and sticky. The tailored trouser suit she was wearing was lightweight, but not lightweight enough. She realised the fingers of one hand were biting like claws into the handle of her briefcàse as she waved goodbye with the other.

She tried Mike on the mobile to let him know she had arrived safely, but there was no signal. She really was alone. Turning to stare at the impressive iron-studded door marking the entrance to Tino's home, she sucked in one more breath, and then ran up the steps.

CHAPTER THREE

LISA realized she was staring foolishly. She had been prepared for most things, but not this. Words refused to form
in response to the young woman's greeting. She could only
fight the rigor in her lips, and bob her head.

The girl couldn't have been much more than twenty-five,
and was tall and very beautiful, with a cloud of inky-black
hair that fell well below her naked shoulders. She was
tanned—evenly, beautifully, naturally tanned—and she
smelled fresh, like sea spray, as if she had just returned
from the beach. She was wearing something floaty and di-
aphanous in muted shades of new-shoot green and lemon,
over what might have been a bikini—it didn't feel right to
look too closely—and her tiny feet were bare with bright
red toenails. And Tino was standing right behind her.

Lisa sensed, rather than saw him. She didn't trust herself
to look. Her head was still reeling. She wasn't taking anything in too clearly... She shouldn't care. Of course she
shouldn't care... She ordered herself angrily to get her head
up—to look him in the eye. When she did, she found that
he was almost a head taller than his beautiful companion,
and that his right hand was resting lightly on the young
woman's waist.

The urge to make some angry, guttural sound at the sight
of that hand—the same hand that had held her so firmly,
the hand that was now resting on another woman—threat-
ened to overwhelm her. Just when she needed all her wits
about her, she was transfixed by that hand, and by Tino's
proprietary air towards a young woman he was showing no
inclination to introduce her to.

She took matters into her own hands 'Hi, my name's Lisa Bond. I've come to see Tino on business—'

'Arianna knows why you're here, Lisa.'

Like the woman he called Arianna, Tino was dressed casually, as if they had come up from the beach together. Lisa found herself gripped by jealousy: irrational, unwelcome, inescapable jealousy. All she could think of was the touch of his hands on her body and that for a split second before she had pushed him away she had almost lost control.

Both Arianna and Tino were so relaxed, their outfits so normal for any couple living by the sea. Tino's bronzed feet were naked, and dusted with sand, his casual shirt barely held in place by a couple of buttons. He must have dressed in a hurry... He could hold one woman so passionately in his arms it was branded on her mind, and then coolly return home to another?

Lisa calmed herself. This was business—no need to make it personal. The only way to get money into the bank fast enough to save Bond Steel was to get that money from a cash-rich company like Zagorakis Inc. Zagorakis had to buy her small engineering works. Her personal feelings were irrelevant. She wasn't going anywhere until the deal was sewn up.

She viewed the couple again, trying to work out what she was up against. There was the wrong dynamic between them for Arianna to be Tino's sister... And then she noticed Tino's bleached linen trousers were rolled up almost to his knees. The sight of his naked legs stirred some very primitive emotions inside her, not least of which was the knowledge that Arianna must know how it would feel to have those powerful legs wrapped around her—

Andreas had warned him she was coming. But this was better than he had expected. Seeing Lisa hovering uncertainly on his doorstep gave him a real rush. It was time she learned she couldn't win every battle in the boardroom, or the bedroom.

She was thrown by the fact that he wasn't alone, and that his companion was a beautiful young woman. Good. That was her first lesson. She was so used to ruling the roost at Bond Steel, she took too much for granted. No one outside his inner circle could say if he had brothers or sisters, or any family at all. Curiosity about Arianna had to be eating her up inside; he planned to keep it that way as long as possible.

Tino's face told Lisa very little. What was he thinking? Chasing after him had put her on the back foot, but the deal was too crucial to the survival of Bond Steel for her to entrust it to a third party. Yes, of course it would have been better for her to deal with him by mail, at a distance— but that just wasn't her way. She never shirked a confrontation. It just hadn't occurred to her that Tino's life might be very different from her own. She should have known that a man like Constantine Zagorakis would never want for female company.

She managed a smile—that encompassed both the people facing her. 'It's very good of you to see me like this.' Arianna smiled back, but Lisa found herself confronting a brick wall in Tino's eyes.

Damn! Damn! Damn! She was only being nice for Arianna's sake. This picture of domestic bliss had really thrown her. She should have known that 'nice' didn't suit her. She had given Tino the advantage over her right away...

She had pictured a butler showing her into a room where there would have been a chance to look around and draw conclusions about the very private Constantine Zagorakis. Those conclusions would have helped her to hone her business strategy. There would have been time to sip a refreshing drink while she lowered the temperature in her heart to freezing just to remind herself that the idea of courting Clifton Steel must have been in his mind all the time he'd been holding her, leading her on to the point where he'd almost kissed her.

A few steadying breaths and she could feel her determination flowing back. She was over her jealousy, and ready to concentrate on rescuing the deal. On bettering him, on triumphing over the bastard!

'You're always welcome, Lisa.'

Always welcome? Was he mocking her now?

'Andreas told us to expect you.'

'It won't take long.' Lisa glanced apologetically at Arianna. She refused to see the young woman as a rival, if only because that would have meant Tino had some sort of hold over her. 'I'm staying at the Zagorakis guest house,' she added in case he should think she was looking for board and lodgings. She had the satisfaction of seeing his gaze sharpen.

'Tino, please—' Arianna touched his arm '—Lisa looks so pale. She must be tired. She's had a long journey.'

Pale and tired? Pale because she was strung out like a wire, perhaps...

'Arianna's right. Won't you come in, Lisa?'

Was the humour in his voice only apparent to her? Lisa wondered as she went past them both into the house. She would have to handle this carefully. It might be just a game to him, but she had no intention of losing Bond Steel to Tino Zagorakis.

The hallway was magnificent. It couldn't have been a more perfect setting for two such beautiful people. A plant-filled atrium stretched towards a stained glass cupola set into the roof, and where the dying rays of the sun penetrated it caused jewels of light to tremble on the floor beneath her feet.

Something made her turn and she noticed Arianna slipping away. Doubtless all Tino's women would be equally well trained. They would have to become used to coming second to his business interests.

Beneath the curve of an impressive staircase she spotted a grand piano—it surprised her if only because it wasn't there for show. The lid was raised, and there was a selection of music littering the stand, as well as the floor around the piano stool..Bartók, Bach, Liszt and Brahms, all challenging, cerebral pieces, with a strong dose of romance in the mix…

'Are you interested in music, Lisa?'

She could feel Tino's stare burning into her back. 'Yes, I am, as it happens.'

'Does it surprise you to find music here?'

'Surprise me? No.' No one knew anything about Constantine Zagorakis, or the way he lived, but she was intrigued by the music, and felt sure it must belong to someone else. Zagorakis didn't possess the heart for music. 'Does your friend play the piano?'

'Are you talking about Arianna?'

Lisa shrugged. She didn't want him mistaking her interest for good old-fashioned female jealousy. 'Yes, I wondered if the music belonged to Arianna.'

'Arianna plays the piano occasionally—but more to learn her parts than anything else. She's an opera singer by profession.'

'I see.' Why didn't that surprise her? Was it because there was something about the dark-eyed beauty that reminded her of her idol, the late diva suprema, Maria Callas? There was the same passion and the same intensity in Arianna's expression. Was there the same heartbreak courtesy of a Greek billionaire in store for her too?

'Does Arianna do lot of travelling?' Do you travel with her? Or do you play away when she's working?

Tino made a noncommittal sound, and she wasn't about to repeat the question. And now he was holding open a door she saw led into his study. She had been so busy with her own thoughts, she hadn't realised they had arrived at their destination.

His study was cool, though surprisingly cosy. The cushions were designed to sink into, and the lighting was subtle. Two sofas were arranged either side of a large stone fireplace, but the fire wasn't lit as the weather was too warm. The windows were open and she could hear the insistent chirrup of cicadas through the slim, slatted blinds.

'Make yourself comfortable, Lisa.'

'Thank you.' She hadn't realised how weary she was, but much depended on this visit and she couldn't afford to lose concentration. She had to secure the deal. She had to save Bond Steel, whatever the personal cost. She couldn't let Tino take the company as easily as he had stolen her self-control.

He invited her to sit down.

'I'll go and get some drinks. White wine all right?'

Wine? To soften her up? She still rued the champagne she had shared with him on Thursday night. 'Just water for me, please.'

As Tino left the room Lisa knew, however well prepared she was, there were certain things she couldn't know. How far down the road was his deal with Clifton? Could she still convince Zagorakis that her small engineering works was the best option for him, and that he didn't need the aggravation of two larger companies like Bond and Clifton?

Doubt washed over her to the point where she wondered if her fighting juices were all used up—and then the door swung open and he walked in. 'Does Arianna know who you were with on Thursday night?'

'I doubt she'd be interested.'

As Tino stared at her Lisa wondered what was she doing making any of this personal—the one thing she had vowed not to do. But, however cold-bloodedly she approached the situation, a very female part of her wanted answers. Watching him open a bottle of Chablis, she wished things could have been simpler between them. If they had been she would have asked him who the hell Arianna was, and get it over with.

There was a jug of iced water on the tray as well as a bowl of fresh fruit, and there was also a plate of what looked suspiciously like home-made cookies. Lisa hadn't eaten a thing since breakfast, and now she realised how hungry she was. But how could she eat cookies when foremost in her mind was an image of Arianna playing earth mother for Tino in the kitchen?

Tino made the torture worse, biting into one of them and then uttering a deep-throated sound of pleasure. The last time she had heard him make a sound like that was when he'd almost kissed her—

'Won't you have one?' He held out the plate.

Apart from wanting to crack it over his head, no way was she going to touch it. Tino was so cool, so together, she wanted the cookies to glue his teeth together, or pull them out, or, better still, stick in his throat and choke him.

'Do try one.' He kept on watching her. 'I can assure you, they're delicious.'

'Thank you, no.' She waved them away with an impatient gesture. 'Care to tell me why you're cosying up to Clifton?'

'Ever the businesswoman, Lisa?' He shook his head as he put the plate down on the table. 'You're such fun to be with.'

'I can be.'

'Really? And when would that be?'

The verbal slap came out of nowhere. It took a moment to recover. It seemed Tino shared none of her scruples about avoiding personal issues.

'You have a proposition for me,' he prompted.

'If you're interested?'

'I'm always prepared to listen to a business proposal.'

'I hear you've gone cold on our deal and transferred your interest to Clifton Steel?'

'I'm always looking for possibilities.'

'Have you ruled out my small engineering works?'

He kept her waiting so long Lisa wondered if he'd heard the question.

'I haven't ruled anything out yet,' he said at last.

'I do have other people waiting.'

'Really? Your company's in big trouble Lisa—your share price is falling through the floor.'

'And I'll recover the situation.'

'In time?'

'Yes, if we can reach an agreement.'

'And if you go to one of these *other* companies—can they come up with the cash in time to save Bond Steel?'

'Probably not—' She didn't have the luxury of time to play cat and mouse with him. Reaching into her own brief-case, Lisa welcomed the chance to break eye contact. Tino's stare was so penetrating he made her feel naked—and she needed a clear head to do business with him. 'If you will just take a look at the figures I've been working on…'

'You've been busy—' He lifted the heavy sheaf of documents out of her hands.

Lisa watched tensely as he flicked through them, pausing occasionally to read one or other of the passages more intently. Finally laying them down on the table between them, he sat back again and folded his arms behind his head.

'You need me, Lisa.'

Her business head urged caution. There had been no other serious offers. Zagorakis Inc was cash rich. Tino could write a cheque right now if it came to it. He was the best, her only chance to save Bond Steel. 'What do you think now you've seen the numbers?'

'I'd need to study these a little longer before I give you my final answer, but—'

'OK, I'm listening.'

'Not so fast.' He straightened up, his expression hardening. 'It's me who's listening, Lisa. It's up to you to convince me that your proposal has merit.'

All the people relying on her to secure the deal flashed in front of Lisa's eyes. 'I'll give you a brief run-down of the facts—'

'No. You're not getting the point. You've come here—disturbing me on my island…at my home. This is going to be on my terms, not yours. I'll be generous. I'll give you a working week to convince me that your scheme has merit. If you're successful I'll buy your small engineering works, and bail you out. If you fail the deal is off and everything's in play: Clifton, as well as Bond Steel—'

'No. Bond Steel's not for sale.'

'If you don't deal with me—we both know it will go under.'

'So, that's it,' Lisa accused tensely. 'You're just playing with me. I don't believe you're even going to look at those figures. You'll keep me here where I'm safely out of the picture, and sit it out until Bond Steel goes down.'

'And I can pick it up for practically nothing?' He shrugged in agreement. 'You know that's good business, Lisa—and don't forget I've given you an opportunity to change my mind.'

'Five days? Five days to secure the future of my employees? You can't toy with people like that. And don't try telling me that jobs will be secure under your ownership. If you get your hands on Bond Steel, you'll strip the assets and tip people out of work without a second thought—' She shook her head. 'I was wrong about you—I thought you had some small spark of humanity, but you don't have any feelings at all, do you?'

'None.' It was true. There was very little he could get fired up about. Lisa Bond came close—but she was a page in his life he would turn very soon. He cared about his assets because they funded the project closest to his heart, and he cared about two very special and unique women. Apart from that, feelings were a luxury reserved for other people.

'I'm not staying here to listen any more to this.'

He glanced at her as she got to her feet. 'Then lose your business, Lisa.'

What alternative did she have? However much it hurt, she had to swallow her pride. She made some rapid calculations. 'I'll need internet access, and a phone that works.'

'You're in no position to dictate terms to me.'

'I have to keep in contact with my people. We work as a team.'

'Then it will be interesting for your team to see how well their leader operates without them. It's up to you, Lisa. Go home now, and the deal is off. Send the jet back without you, and there might still be a chance. We'll never know unless you stay.'

'But if you agree to purchase the company our lawyers will need to know—contracts will have to be drawn up.'

'True. So you will phone your PA now and tell him to wait to hear from Andreas, my PA.' Lifting a phone from its square black nest, Tino pushed it across the desk to her. 'Satellite,' he explained in answer to Lisa's questioning look. 'You won't get a signal for your mobile here.'

'So you're going to be the only one who can contact the outside world?'

'That's how it works. If I judge matters are coming to a head, it will be up to me to call the meeting. Now, are you going to make that call, or not?'

Right now it seemed unlikely that such a meeting would ever be called, and, if it was called, she had won. 'All right, I agree.'

He already knew the small works was profitable, but it pleased him to see how far he could push. She had set herself against him. She had made it a battle of wills. She had no idea what she had unleashed. It was his way, or no way. Always.

It was constantly at the back of his mind that if he gave the smallest concession he risked pulling a stitch that might cause his whole life to unravel. He had climbed out of the gutter; he had no intention of slipping back there.

She had to go through with it. It was that or lose the deal.

He watched her as she made the call, reassured her PA and gave him the necessary information. She handled it well. In a tight spot she was cool.

'Thank you for the call,' she said, pushing the phone back across the desk towards him.

'Where do you think you're going?'

'I'm staying at your guest house in the village.'

'There's no need to do that.'

'What do you mean?'

'You'll be staying here.'

'Here? With you at the villa?'

'There's no need to sound quite so unimpressed.'

'But Arianna—'

'Will do as I say.'

Lisa tensed with anger, and it was mostly on Arianna's

behalf. She felt no envy for the young woman now, only pity.

'That's my final offer, Lisa. Take it, or get back on your jet and get out of here.'

That wasn't an option for her, Lisa realized; too many people were depending on her to get this right. She couldn't just walk away. 'All right, I'll stay. But on the understanding that we only meet for business—'

'I told you before you're in no position to make terms, Lisa. This is my island, and I decide when and where we hold our meetings—'

'So, I don't have any say at all?'

She didn't like that. Tough. Being nice to him for five whole days was the most refined torture he could have devised for her. 'Don't let me keep you, Lisa—' He gestured towards the door. 'You can use the internal phones in your suite to order any food you would like—and have it delivered to your room.'

Lisa knew her cheeks were glowing bright red with humiliation. She might have said she didn't want to socialise with him, but she had never thought he would confine her to her room. For a moment she wondered why he hadn't agreed to her staying at the guest house. That way he would have kept her out of Arianna's way... But, of course, at Villa Aphrodite she was out of everyone's reach... completely isolated, completely alone. 'I have to go back to the village to collect my things. So why don't I just stay at the guest house, as I planned?'

'That is not part of our agreement—'

'But you said five days—a working week, Tino. Today is Sunday, so surely our negotiations won't begin until tomorrow morning?'

'It is dangerous to make presumptions in business, Lisa. You should know that—'

Lisa's mouth hardened into an angry line as she stared

at him. So that was the way it was to be. 'I imagined you would extend the usual business courtesies.'

'And so I will from tomorrow. In the meantime, you will stay here.'

'As your prisoner?'

'Don't be ridiculous! I'm not holding you against your will. You know as well as I do that until a deal is struck we must abide by all the terms of the agreement, and not just the ones that suit us most. You have five days as my guest to convince me that I should do this deal. Hardly an ordeal, I would have thought.'

There was a gentle tap on the door, and Lisa welcomed the distraction as the study door opened, and an elderly servant walked in.

'Goodnight, Lisa.'

Her mouth fell open as Tino walked out of the room.

'May I show you to your suite, Thespinis Bond?'

Lisa softened her expression in case she scared the elderly man half to death. 'Thank you, that's very kind of you.'

'It is my pleasure, Thespinis Bond.'

His voice was gentle, and he stood back politely at the door to let her pass. How could such a man bear to work for Tino Zagorakis? Lisa wondered as she followed his elderly retainer across the hall.

The suite of rooms where she was to stay was fabulous. Taking the colours of the Greek flag as inspiration, the furnishings were mostly snowy white with the occasional highlight of cerulean. But before she had chance to properly appreciate the opulence of her surroundings, Lisa's gaze was captured by the sight of her overnight case standing at the end of the bed. Only the presence of Tino's gentle servant prevented her from turning on her heel and going to rip the head off his employer. It was obvious that whether she had agreed to stay or not, Tino had already decided that she would, and had taken it upon himself to retrieve her luggage from the guest house.

'Kirie Zagorakis thought you might prefer to eat out here alone.'

Lisa looked across the room to where the old man was smiling at her. Floor-to-ceiling white muslin curtains billowed gently in the early evening breeze, drawing her attention to the balcony beyond. It was bathed in soft light from some out-of-view lanterns, and she could see that a comfortable chair with a deeply padded cushion awaited her, as well as a dining table, ostentatiously laid out for one.

I bet he did, she thought grimly. Tino had decided she was to be cut off from the rest of the household. She smiled at her elderly companion. He was hardly to blame for his employer's machiavellian scheme. 'Thank you. That's exactly what I'd like.'

Not only had Tino made the unilateral decision that she would stay at Villa Aphrodite, he had delivered instructions to the kitchen for her supper, Lisa discovered when the elderly man showed her the buffet trolley. He must have done that when he'd left the study briefly to get them both a drink, she realised tensely.

'You have such a beautiful view from here, Thespinis Bond.'

The elderly man was pointing out across the cliff tops to where the ocean had turned coppery pink in the last rays of the sun.

'I doubt I've ever seen anything more beautiful,' Lisa said honestly. She was rewarded by the old man's smile…but then she noticed another, larger table had been laid out immediately below and a little in front of her own balcony. The edges of a white lace tablecloth were fluttering gently in the early evening breeze, and crystal and silverware were glittering in the light of flickering candles.

And now she heard the sounds of muted conversation, as well as laughter—high, tinkling laughter, as well as a lower, appreciative sound.

'Would you like to sit down now, Thespinis Bond? Shall I light the candle for you?'

Lisa turned abruptly, realising her elderly companion was still waiting for her to say something. Having struck a match, he was waiting for her permission to light a slim ivory candle. 'No, no,' she said, hurrying over to him. 'Thank you, but I think I'll wait a little. You've been very kind,' she added, seeing his crestfallen face.

Inside she was a morass of anger and humiliation, but there was no way she was going to vent her feelings on an innocent old man. It made no sense that she cared about Tino's dining arrangements, but she did—it hurt a lot. Not only had Tino chosen to dine without her, he was dining with someone else…almost certainly Arianna.

'Are you sure that is all you require from me this evening, Thespinis Bond?'

'I'm quite sure. Thank you.' Lisa smiled again, and waited until the elderly man had closed the door behind him. She would not sit obediently on her solitary perch and take the humiliation Tino had planned for her. She would feel it. Oh, yes, just as he had known, she would feel it, but she would do so in private…

Carefully loading all the supper dishes onto the trolley, Lisa rolled it towards her room. Wheeling it inside, she firmly closed the double doors behind her.

CHAPTER FOUR

LISA slept more soundly than she had expected. It had to be the sea air, she reasoned, waking slowly. Dawn was just peeping through the white muslin drapes as she stretched like a cat in the sun. At first she was reluctant to leave the warm linen sheets, but then she remembered everything that had happened the previous night.

Slipping out of bed, she padded barefoot across the cool tiled floor and opened the double doors onto the balcony. Today was Monday, the first day of her five-day trial, and she had no intention of wasting a single minute—but she could make time for this. She had guessed the view would be spectacular in daylight, but she had never imagined it could be quite so lovely.

Shading her eyes against the low-slanting sunlight, she realised the villa sat on a promontory with the ocean to three sides. The water far below the cliffs was graded in colour from a white lace frill at the shoreline to palest blue at the midline, and then on to deepest Prussian blue where the ocean floor dropped away.

The gardens surrounding the villa were equally stunning. They combined formal and informal planting with great success, and were ablaze with colour. Beyond the stone patio she could see an infinity pool. She had hoped for a pool, and was longing for a swim, but there was already someone swimming there…

Meeting up with Tino when they were both half naked was a bad idea—but hadn't the taxi driver mentioned steps leading to the beach, and even a funicular running down the face of the cliff? There had to be a way she could get to the sea without walking past the pool...

Unzipping her overnight case, Lisa plucked out the bikini she had packed in the hope of snatching a few moments in the Greek sunshine. Fortunately, she had remembered to bring her flip-flops too, as well as a wrap.

The stone steps were steep and worn away in some places, and Lisa was glad of the wooden handrail fixed to the rock. When she reached the halfway point she paused to look around and catch her breath. She gazed longingly at the tracks marking the path the funicular would take. If she could have taken that route she would have been down on the shore by now, but the cabin had been too close to the swimming pool for her to risk it, and the mechanism would have alerted Tino immediately had she been foolish enough to try.

The beach formed a tempting silvery crescent, and the sea had turned to turquoise, and seemed completely flat. Fingers of cloud stretched across the brightening horizon, and the air was sweetly scented. Best of all, there was no sign of Tino, so she could relax and the new day was hers for the taking...

Jumping down onto the beach, Lisa kicked off her flip-flops and dug her toes into the damp sand. It felt wonderful against her warm skin. Tugging off her wrap, she tossed it away and ran eagerly towards the sea.

A much older woman followed Lisa's plunge into the sea with interest. The moment Lisa turned for shore she dipped down to collect the discarded wrap, and then walked down the sand to meet her.

Shaking her long chestnut hair out behind her like a banner, Lisa turned her face to the sun as she ploughed happily through the shallows. She never had time for a holiday, or even for a good swim. Feeling the sunshine on her face, and the tingle of the cool Aegean on her skin, was almost worth braving Tino's lair for—

'*Yia Sou.*'

Having thought she was alone, Lisa nearly jumped out of her skin at the friendly greeting. She recovered quickly, smiling her thanks as the elderly Greek woman handed over her wrap. '*Kalimera.*'

'It is going to be a beautiful day,' the older woman observed, gazing up into the sky.

For you, perhaps, Lisa thought, remembering her meeting later that morning with Tino. 'Yes, it is,' she agreed politely.

'My name is Stella. I live over there in that small cottage…' The woman pointed to a quaint whitewashed building with bright blue shutters and front door, set back a little from the beach. 'I watched you swimming. You are good.'

'Thank you.'

'Won't you join me for breakfast?' Stella gazed down at the basket of freshly baked bread swinging from her arm.

Lisa's stomach rumbled on cue, and they both laughed.

'That's very kind of you.' Lisa was thankful to have found someone so friendly. Anything was preferable to eating breakfast alone on her balcony, where she knew she would only brood on the outcome of her meeting with Tino.

'We will both join you, *Ya-ya.*'

'Tino!' Lisa stood back as the two embraced.

Stella was clearly overjoyed to see him, but Lisa resented the fact that her own face was burning. Why was it Tino always made her feel as if she had done something wrong? It was his behaviour that was outrageous. He was wearing a sun-bleached blue vest and frayed cut-off shorts, and might as well have been naked for all the toned, bronzed flesh on show. His feet were bare, and there was a dusting of sand on his limbs as if he had found time for a swim in the sea as well as his morning workout in the pool…while she was wearing a scanty bikini beneath a filmy wrap—not her battle clothes of choice.

'Good morning, Lisa. I trust you slept well?'

'I did, thank you.' Lisa glanced at Stella, hoping she hadn't picked up the undercurrents between them.

'I have plenty of food for all of us. Come,' Stella insisted, beckoning them towards her cottage.

There was a tug of amusement at one corner of Tino's mouth, Lisa noticed as she hurried after Stella, and however she tried to mistime her stride he managed to keep in step with her. 'I suppose you just happened by?' Her tone was frosty.

'Actually, I came to see Stella.'

Lisa's curiosity flared. 'Do you know her well?'

'We've known each other for a number of years.'

'I see.'

'I doubt it.'

The murmured comment stirred her interest even more. Who was Stella? And what was her connection with the most obnoxious man on the planet?

Having reached her front door, Stella opened it and beckoned them inside.

The interior was cool and shady with slivers of sunlight slanting in through the shutters. The air smelled faintly of herbs, and, gazing around, Lisa noticed that every window ledge was lined with terracotta pots sprouting densely packed greenery. 'What a lovely home you have.'

Stella smiled, pointing to the easy chairs. 'Please, both of you sit down.'

'Are you sure I can't help you with anything?' Lisa said, ignoring this suggestion as she edged towards the kitchen door.

'No, no.' Stella was quite certain on this point. 'You two relax, and let me prepare the food. I won't take long.'

You two? Again she was bracketed with the last man on

earth she would have chosen to be paired with. Lisa would have thought the distance that existed between them would have been glaringly obvious to everyone, especially to a woman who seemed as bright and observant as Stella. Wandering across the room, she casually picked out a window seat as far away from Tino as possible. Sitting down, she stared out through the barely open shutter.

'Is that better for you?'

Lisa breathed in convulsively as Tino leaned across to open the shutters a little more for her. She could feel his warmth in every fibre of her being. And then he remained at her side so that the acute, and very troubling, awareness of him refused to fade.

'You're an early riser, Lisa.'

'I always wake at dawn on a working day.' Her voice was clipped, inviting no further conversation between them. And then, to Lisa's relief, Stella bustled back into the room carrying a loaded breakfast tray.

'Why didn't you call me to bring this in for you?' Tino demanded, crossing the room in a couple of strides to take the tray from her.

'Because you were keeping our visitor company.' Stella stared hard at him before releasing the tray, and then she turned to Lisa. 'Forgive me, Lisa, I am sure you do not want to hear us bickering.'

'You know my name?' Lisa frowned, realising she had forgotten to introduce herself. She glanced at Tino, but he was suddenly too busy unloading the breakfast tray to notice. 'I'm sorry, Stella, I should have said.' Lisa made up for her earlier lapse with a smile, 'I'm Lisa Bond. I'm here to do business with Tino.'

'Business with Tino?' Pulling a face, Stella made a fanning motion with her hand that required no translation.

'I'm sure I can handle him.' Lisa stared at him so that he could be in no doubt that she would.

'So, what are your plans today?' Stella looked between them as she piled their plates high with fresh bread and honey.

'We have a meeting.'

'I plan to take Lisa out on the boat.'

They both spoke at once, and Lisa bridled instantly. She had no intention of wasting the first of her five precious negotiating days on Tino's floating gin palace.

'And I will bring back some fresh fish for your supper,' he added to Stella.

'I shall look forward to it.' Stella clapped her hands with pleasure.

Lisa looked from one to the other. Tino was not going to ignore her. And he was not going to draw this lovely, innocent woman into some devious plan he had concocted. They had more important things to do than catch fish today. She watched angrily as he tucked into his breakfast with relish. Breaking off a crispy crust from one of the chunks of bread, he dipped it in some honey.

'No,' she said flatly.

'No?' Tino paused, bread in hand, to stare at her.

'I'm not coming with you—I have better things to do than idle my time away. I thought we both did.'

'Lisa?' Putting a hand to his chest, Tino affected an innocent expression.

'Don't you like boats?' Stella looked concerned.

'It isn't that.' Lisa hesitated. What could she say without causing an atmosphere? 'I'm just not used to doing business—'

'The Greek way?' Stella suggested helpfully.

A glance at Tino was enough to convince Lisa that he couldn't have been more pleased with the way things were turning out if he had scripted the exchange himself.

'All Greek men are fishermen at heart, Lisa,' Stella explained kindly, unaware of the tension stretching between her visitors. 'It's better if you just go along with their way of doing business.'

'I'm sure you're right, Stella,' Lisa said politely, not wanting to cause offence.

'What was that? What did you say?' Tino could hardly keep the smile off his face.

'If you'd been listening, you'd know,' Lisa said tartly, and then froze. Stella's face was a picture, and no wonder. She could hardly have expected her breakfast guests to start yelling at each other.

For a moment there was an uncomfortable silence, which Tino did nothing to break. Then, slowly turning back to his breakfast, he dipped another piece of bread into the honey.

Lisa felt she had to say something by way of explanation for her behaviour. 'I'm so sorry, Stella. I don't know what came over me.'

'Think nothing of it.' Stella dismissed the moment with a smile. 'Tempers flare high when passions are roused.'

Passions! Passions? Lisa glared at Tino. Whatever Stella imagined, she was wrong—absolutely wrong.

'Tino has always aroused strong passions in people,' Stella added.

She couldn't let this go on, Lisa realised, holding up her hands in front of her. 'There's absolutely no chance of Tino upsetting my equilibrium, Stella. It's just that—'

'It's just what, Lisa?' Tino demanded softly, unfolding from his chair.

As Lisa's mouth opened to shoot back a reply he fed a piece of honey-soaked crust between her lips. 'Suck on this,' he suggested in an undertone. 'You could do with sweetening up.'

Having no option but to chew, and then swallow, Lisa channelled her fury into her eyes, which locked with his fiercely.

* * *

Lisa had been marching along in silence since they had left the cottage, but now they were out of earshot she could speak her mind. 'I'm not going another step.'

Tino glanced back at her without slowing. 'It's not too far away now. The harbour is just over there, around the base of the cliff.'

'It's not the distance that worries me.'

'What, then?' He ground to a halt, and turned to stare at her.

'Stop this, Tino. I'm not going out on your boat. We both know you've got me over a barrel, but, if you have any decency left in you at all, you'd come back with me to the villa and hold our meeting like you promised—'

'Not now, Lisa.'

'What do you mean, not now?'

'I mean I don't want to discuss business right now?' He put his face very close so she was forced to take a step back.

'But once the deal is wrapped up we can go our separate ways,' she pointed out, 'which I know you want as much as I do.'

'Once the deal is wrapped up?' He stared at her mockingly. 'You're very sure of yourself.'

'I'm confident that I've come up with the right deal for you?'

He laughed, throwing his head back. 'So now you've got my best interests at heart? I don't think so, Lisa.'

'All right.' She was forced to hurry after him when he started down the path again. 'So we both need this deal.'

'I don't need anything from you.'

'Really? So why are your people scurrying around trying to buy up everything in sight?'

That stopped him.

'Maybe it pleases me to know that I can.'

'I'm very happy for you, but my life is rather more complicated. I have loyalties.'

'You have an overabundance of pride…and a highly inflated opinion of yourself.'

'That's rich coming from you!'

'And if the tables were turned, you'd treat me differently? No. So don't expect any leeway from me, when you'd give me none yourself.' He turned back to the path, forcing her to run after him again.

'But you gave me your word that this week would be devoted to our negotiations.'

'On my terms.' He didn't pause, or look back.

'All right.' Lisa stopped running. Resting her hands on her knees, she tried to catch her breath.

'All right, what?'

At least he had stopped. He was standing a few yards away, waiting for her to say something. She fought for control. But as she straightened up her feelings erupted. 'I suppose Arianna is happy about our little pleasure cruise?'

'Arianna isn't your concern.'

'How convenient for you.'

'Why are you worrying about Arianna?'

'Someone needs to. I feel sorry for her.'

'Why, exactly?'

'I think you know why, Tino.'

'No, I don't. I'm waiting to hear what you have to say about it.'

'All right, then… What the hell are we doing here?' She gestured around. 'We should go back to the villa and have our meeting under proper conditions. All this is far too distracting.'

'I thought that part of our agreement was that I decide when and where our meetings are held.'

'But we can't have them here.'

'Exactly.' His voice was maddeningly controlled.

'You're becoming forgetful, Lisa. I already told you that we are not holding any meetings today.'

'So, you're breaking your word?'

'I don't remember saying we wouldn't be holding any meetings this week. You shouldn't have agreed to something before you were certain of the terms.'

'Don't you dare lecture me on business etiquette. I agreed to your terms before I realised how irresponsible you were going to be.'

'Irresponsible?'

'Yes,' Lisa insisted fiercely. 'Irresponsible. Now, can we stop wasting time, and get back to the villa? I want a shower—I'm all salty. We can still get in a couple of hours of discussions before lunch... What do you think you're doing?' She glared down at the hand on her arm. 'Don't you dare touch me!'

But he was already propelling her along the path.

'I'm warning you—'

'And I'm telling you,' he fired back, dragging her in front of him to stare into her eyes. 'I make the decisions here, and today business is off the agenda. You heard me tell Stella I'd get her some fish for her supper? Well, that takes precedence over anything else.'

'You're going fishing?' Lisa demanded incredulously.

'No, Lisa—we're going fishing.'

Before Lisa could stop him he swung her off the ground, and held her so tightly she couldn't fight him off.

'If I say we're going out on the boat, we're going out on the boat,' he informed her as he strode along. 'And if I choose to take hold of your arm, I take hold of your arm. Do you understand me any better yet, Lisa?'

'I understand you're a brute—and you'd better put me down right now, or face the consequences.'

'Consequences? What consequences are those, Lisa?' His pace didn't falter. 'Are you going to set your lawyers onto my legal team? Because I strongly advise you to think twice before you do that..unless, of course, you want to be begging me to give you a job in a couple of months' time.'

'I wouldn't expect you to give me the dirt from under your fingernails.'

'As I don't have any, you'll have to excuse me if I'm not too worried about that.'

'Are you going to put me down—or shall I scream?'

'Scream all you want..no one will hear you.' They'll only think we're having fun. You're not going to win this one—accept it.'

Lisa kicked her legs furiously in reply. 'This isn't a joke, Tino.'

'What's your problem? Are you still worried about Arianna? Or are you more worried about being alone with me?'

Lisa gave a short, scornful laugh. 'Yes, I am worried about Arianna—but as for you?' She looked at him with disdain. 'I couldn't give a damn about you.'

Dropping her to the ground, he held her at arm's length, the tension flaring between them. 'No need to descend to the language of the gutter, young woman.'

'To describe you?' Lisa couldn't believe she was shouting. 'I'd say it's absolutely necessary.'

'And if I told you Arianna and I aren't a couple?'

'I'd be happy, relieved—for her. And I'd still want to go back to the villa. No contact between us other than for business, remember that, Tino?'

'So, we shouldn't do this, for instance...'

The breath shot out of Lisa's lungs as he dragged her close. Feelings exploded out of her. And it wasn't the fact that Tino was kissing her that went storming through her brain, it was the fact that she loved it. He felt good, better than good. Making rough, animal sounds, she moved passionately against him. But as he moulded her even closer to him she hated him—hated him for making her want him so badly it hurt, so badly her legs were giving way beneath her.

She came to her senses abruptly. Bond Steel's future depended on her, and this was how she behaved? Tino was only playing games with her, and while she was distracted his troops were swarming all over her business.

She started fighting him then. She fought his mouth, his lips, his tongue, and she grappled with his hands, making sounds of fury in her throat. But he had her bound so tightly against him, she could hardly breathe, let alone break free. And then, just when she felt she had no more fight left in her, he let her go, and stood back.

'So this is your idea of persuasion?' he said.

'It's a lot more honest than kissing you back.' Turning her face away from him, she held her forehead with her hand. 'I can't believe I'm in this position. I hate you so much.'

'No,' Tino countered steadily. 'What you hate is the way I make you lose control.'

'I know what I mean.'

'Dangerous ground, Lisa. You know what they say about hate.'

'Don't flatter yourself!'

'I don't.'

Lisa made an angry sound. 'So, I'm stuck with this for the next week?'

'If you mean me.. then, yes, you are.'

'Well, don't ever try that again,' she warned. 'And d give me that look either. I'm warning you...I m Tino.'

'Of course you do.'

Tino knew what was at stake for her, Lisa like it or not, she was tied in to this. Tino the fate of Bond Steel in the palm of his hand, and she had to play by his rules, or risk losing everything.

He stood watching her, slouched on one hip. 'Do you know what you need?' His voice had turned low and mocking.

'No, but I'm sure you're going to tell me.'

'You need someone to say no to you, Lisa—someone who can curb your headstrong ways.'

'Headstrong?' She'd never put a foot wrong in all her adult life—and no one in his right mind would call her headstrong. No one would dare. 'And I suppose you think you're man enough for the job?'

'I know I am.'

The sardonic murmur made Lisa shiver with desire. She had to fight it, fight him. 'I've had enough of this. I want to go back.'

'Not a chance,' he said flatly. 'We are going to enter into negotiations Greek style.'

'What are you talking about? Greek style?' Ancient tableaux of partly clothed men and women captured in various poses of sensual indulgence sprang into Lisa's mind. She was prepared to go a long way to secure the deal, but not that far.

'We're going to get properly acquainted before we sit round a table.'

'Properly acquainted?' Her throat squeezed tight. 'Why? I don't want to.'

'Bad luck for your company.' He shook his head.

'No—stop…wait a minute.' To Lisa's relief he stopped walking and turned around.

'So, we're agreed?' he said. 'No more talk of business day?'

She muttered two words grudgingly: 'All right.'

'That's good, Lisa.'

Did he have to make it sound as if she had achieved something monumental?

'That wasn't so hard, now, was it?'

Lisa confined herself to a glare.

'There can be no possibility of a deal until I find you more biddable.'

'Biddable?' That was too much! 'So, now you're resorting to blackmail?'

'Blackmail?' Shaking his head, Tino made a sound of disappointment with his tongue against the roof of his mouth. He was teasing her, taunting her—baiting her. 'No, not blackmail, Lisa. You see, if you respond well, I will be fair. But if you are determined to remain wilful and contrary, then you will have to be tamed.'

'Tamed? I'd like to see you try.'

'Is that a challenge, Lisa?'

And then, incredibly, before she realised what he meant to do, he had picked her up and put her over his knee! And before she could recover from that, he exclaimed, '*Theos!* You would send me mad!' And let her tumble to the ground as if her naked flesh had scorched him.

Wiping a hand over his eyes, Tino looked as if he couldn't believe what had happened. Scrambling to her feet, Lisa couldn't believe it either. She didn't know whether to rail at him, or laugh, and the longer they stood staring at each other, the more she wanted to laugh.

Tino was clearly stunned that a moment of passion had brought him to the point where he had almost put her over his knee and spanked her, while she was surprised the idea excited her so much. She had to think fast. She couldn't let this drive a wedge between them or it would be the end of the deal. 'We both need some cooling-off time.' Nervous laughter bubbled out of her, but Tino's expression stopped it dead.

What was this turning into? Tino stared at Lisa hard. He

had never come close to losing control before, but right now his senses were raging. In an ideal world, sex between them would have been fun—explosive—but the courtly dance of civilised behaviour stood between them. That and his determination to bring her to heel. But he realised now that where the thought of subduing a woman physically was anathema to him, the thought of spanking Lisa as a prelude to something else was overwhelmingly appealing.

'Are you all right?' His voice sounded gruff in his ears. 'All right?'

He braced himself for the explosion he was sure would come, but when she held his gaze her eyes were sparkling brighter than he'd ever seen them…

She wanted him.

He kept his face neutral, though right now his mind was in turmoil. He was relieved to know he hadn't frightened her, but this wasn't a game to him any more..or, if it was, the rules had just changed, because he wanted Lisa Bond more than he had ever wanted anything in his life before…and that made him deeply uneasy.

CHAPTER FIVE

FOR a few seconds the air between them crackled with intensity. It wasn't just Tino who had been carried away, Lisa realized; she had been too. The thought of a physical tussle with a man as strong as Tino ending in something that didn't involve violence was going to play on her mind for a long time to come. If she could trust a man enough...if she could trust Tino enough...if it could be safe. She'd never been with a man before, had always been so scared. Now, all she felt was aroused and very tempted.

'I'm going fishing,' Tino said brusquely, breaking into her thoughts. 'Are you coming with me, or not?'

Lisa glanced down at her salt-caked self.

'We can get some things for you down at the port.'

'Wait,' she called as he started down the path. 'What are you talking about? What things?'

He stopped, and turned around. 'Sun cream, a hat...nothing to get too excited about. Come on, then—we've wasted enough time.'

'Can we talk business on the boat?'

'You never give up, do you, Lisa?'

'No.'

He stopped so abruptly she almost bumped into him. 'Do you need forty hours to convince me?'

'Of course I don't.'

'Then what are you worried about?' He started off in the direction of the harbour again.

'I'm not worried,' she shouted after him.

'Really?' He lengthened his stride.

'Cold-blooded *son of a bitch*,' Lisa muttered as she hurried after him.

The local store stocked most essentials, and a straw hat with a wide brim was soon found for her, as well as some high factor sun cream—two bottles.

'You're very fair-skinned,' Tino said as he pressed them into her hands. 'You must use plenty.'

Lisa bobbed her head, still mutinous. Gazing out to distract herself from Tino's mannish sweep of the store, she saw his yacht towering over the local boats. At least, she presumed it must be his. It was a sleek white colossus amidst all the tiny fishing vessels. 'That's an impressive business perk,' she said when they left the shop.

'I'm glad you like it.'

He was right. She didn't need forty hours to convince him, and when would she get another opportunity to take a cruise on a billionaire's yacht? Lisa was surprised by how childishly excited she was at the prospect. She was even a little impatient when Tino stopped outside another shop and steered her inside.

At the local bakery and general food store, when greetings had been formally exchanged with the beaming host, a wicker basket, not dissimilar to the one Stella had been carrying, was handed to them over the counter.

'Our picnic,' Tino explained, taking charge of it.

'Our picnic?' Lisa frowned. Didn't billionaires carry chefs on their yachts these days?

When Tino walked straight past the gangway to the *Stellamaris Odyssey*, she halted at the foot of it.

'What now?' he grated, turning round.

'But, I thought—'

'Oh, dear—your bottom lip is trembling, Lisa.'

She probably did look like a child whose promised treat had just been snatched away—that was how she felt. 'I didn't want to go fishing in the first place,' she pointed out, pretending not to care.

'Does this look like a fishing boat?' Tino gazed up the sides of his sleek white yacht.

'No, of course not, but I thought—'

'You thought?'

He made it sound like a breakthrough.

'You insisted we must go out on your boat, Tino—'

'No one in their right minds would call the *Stellamaris Odyssey* a boat, Lisa.'

'Oh, well, excuse me! What am I supposed to know about billionaires' toys?'

'This is the woman who owns a jet talking?'

'I don't own a jet; my company owns a jet.'

'Forgive me—I understood you owned Bond Steel?'

'Most of it,' she admitted tightly.

'In my opinion a day out on a luxury yacht is nothing special. I use it for business, and for impressing clients. You don't need to be impressed, do you, Lisa?'

'No, of course not.'

'Excellent, because I've got something rather different planned for you.'

Now he *was* making her nervous…the sexual tension was still crackling. Craning her neck, Lisa tried to see past him. Whatever craft they would be using had to be here somewhere, she reasoned, but the last boat in line after the *Stellamaris Odyssey* was a modest blue and white fishing boat. 'Do you mean that?'

'What's wrong with it? Or is my poor fishing vessel not good enough for you, Your Royal Highness?' He gave her a mock bow.

Holding herself firmly in check, Lisa took one last longing look at the *Stellamaris Odyssey*.

Following her gaze, Tino smiled. 'Oh, no, Lisa, that would be far too self-indulgent. I'm sure you agree that lean and mean is the best way to do business. You do still want to do business with me?'

'Of course I do.'

'In that case, come along—the galley on the fishing boat is rather primitive, and we don't want our wine getting warm.'

It was fun. She hadn't expected that. The day she'd moved in with her father, five-star luxury had become the norm—and even a five-star norm could become boring after a while. Not like this... This was special. The sun was warm on her face, and the breeze tasted salty and fresh...

While Tino took the helm, Lisa stored their provisions in the simple galley before joining him on deck.

'I hope you found the ice. I had someone from the yacht bring it over in a bucket.'

'Don't worry—our wine is now in that bucket.' She wasn't going to let him run away with the idea that she was still disappointed. 'Are you going to tell me where we're heading, or is that still a secret?'

'No secret—somewhere special...somewhere private.'

Private? How well did he intend them to get to know each other? Lisa's heart started pumping. 'How much more private does it get? This is your island, isn't it?'

'Why don't you wait and see?'

Tino was right. The tiny cove they sailed into was completely secluded, and the only sound apart from the rolling surf was the beat of a thousand wings as birds rose in a cloud as they approached. The boat puttered in with its engine idling, and when she leaned over the side Lisa could see tiny fish swooping in vast shoals beneath them. 'Come and see this,' she called excitedly, forgetting the state of their relationship.

Cutting the engine, Tino joined her at the rail. 'We'll have to swim ashore. I can't take her in any closer.'

'What about our food?'

'I'll just drop anchor.'

Lisa turned to watch Tino pad across the deck. He looked like no businessman she'd ever seen before. The ones she was used to dealing with were somewhat lacking on the strong-tanned-leg front...and on the muscular-torso front too.

'Food?' he reminded her when he came back.

'What? Oh, yes, the food.'

'Well? Where is it?'

'In the galley.'

'So, go and get it.' He folded his arms.

It seemed compliance was her lot—for now, Lisa accepted grimly.

'There's a waterproof ice-box in the galley,' Tino called after her as she hurried off. 'Fill it up with our provisions, and then attach the rope you'll find on the shelf. When you've done that, give me a shout, and I'll carry it up.'

'I can manage.'

'I'll carry it up.'

She turned and they stared at each other unblinking.

'I'm just going to check the lobster pots to see if I have a treat to take home for Stella,' he told her steadily, 'and then I'll come down and get the ice-box and carry it up for you.'

When Tino returned he was as good as his word. Leaning over the rail, he carefully lowered the ice-box as close to the sea as the rope would allow. He let it drop the last couple of feet and then sprang onto the side-rail. 'Don't worry, I'll help you up.' Crouching down, he reached out to her.

Take his hand? Not in a million years.

'Have it your way.' He straightened up, balancing easily on the narrow rail as the boat rocked to and fro.

'You mean I've got to dive in...from up there?'

'Unless you'd rather go to the stern and climb down the steps.'

'No. This is fine for me.' Thrusting her hand into Tino's, she let him help her up.

'You'd better take this off before you try to dive in.'

Lisa gasped as he tugged off her wrap. 'That's pretty slick. How many times have you done that before?'

'Do you care?'

'No, of course not.'

Arcing away from her with a grin, he dived backwards into the sea. Breaking the surface, he shook his hair out of his eyes. 'It's your turn now, Lisa. Don't worry, I'm here to save you.'

'Why doesn't that fill me with confidence?' Lisa muttered. Closing her eyes, she didn't hesitate. If she had, she would have been forced to trudge to the stern with her tail between her legs to find the steps.

'That was quite a dive,' Tino said, steadying her as the waves buffeted them against each other.

'Well, I could hardly let you get the better of me.'

'No, indeed.'

He had already slipped the rope from the ice-box over his shoulder, she noticed, trying to avoid brushing against him.

'Are you going to make it to shore all right without me?'

'I should think I can manage.' The sooner she left him, the safer she would be!

'In that case, after you.' Pulling away a couple of strokes, he gave her room to kick out.

This was not what she had imagined when she'd left home, Lisa realised, striking out for the shore. This was the first deal she had negotiated in an aquamarine sea beneath a blazing hot sun with a man like Tino Zagorakis. All the more reason to keep her wits about her.

'You're full of surprises.'

And he did look surprised when she opened the ice-box on the beach. She had just pulled out the sun cream and now her rather squashed hat. 'I'm not a complete numbskull, you know.' She rammed the battered hat onto her head. But as she dipped inside again to find the sun cream so did Tino, putting their faces millimetres apart.

'Would you like me to rub some cream onto your back?'

'No.' Her voice was sharper than she intended as she pulled back abruptly. 'Thank you,' she managed belatedly.

Why had it never occurred to her that they would land up on a beach together practically naked? She should at least have tied her wrap around her waist. As it was they might as well have been two castaways on their own desert island... And now she was blessed with Tino for the whole day, Tino in his customary mocking mood...

Lisa looked away to distract herself. There was an apron of pristine ivory sand, beyond which the land broke up into scrub with a shading of feathery tamarisk trees, and beneath those some gnarled, and not half so friendly, prickly juniper bushes. Wild flowers were scattered about the sand dunes where they were sitting—pink campions, violet sea-lavender...

'Do you like it here?'

'I love it. It's one of the most beautiful places I've ever seen—but then I thought that when I first saw Villa Aphrodite. You're a very lucky man.'

'Luck played no part in it.'

Lisa tensed. Tino's voice had changed. He reminded her of Jack Bond. That was exactly the sort of comment her father would have made.

They ate in silence after that, drinking sharp green wine out of pottery beakers. The olives, soaked in oil, were plump and delicious, and the shopkeeper had included some sweet fat raisins to eat with the crusty bread and goat's cheese. There was even a drawstring muslin bag containing some sugared almonds for their pudding. They reminded Lisa of other people's weddings.

'Almonds and raisins.' Loosening the string on the muslin pack, Tino tipped some of them into his hand, and then added some raisins to the mix. 'The bitter and the sweet, just like life.'

Lisa seized the opportunity. 'About Arianna...'

Lisa noticed how closed Tino's expression had become. There was definitely more to his relationship with Arianna than he was letting on. She was right to probe.

'I've told you all you need to know about Arianna.'

'You told me that she was Stella's daughter, but—'

'But what? What more do you want to know about her, Lisa?'

Not just Arianna.. *you* and Arianna. 'I'm not sure yet.'

'Yet?' He stared at her thoughtfully for a moment, and then his eyes brightened with understanding. At the same time one corner of his mouth tugged up in his trademark annoying half-smile. 'Do you think I've brought you here to pounce on you?'

'I think you've got marginally more style than that.'

'That's very kind of you—and for your information, I have known Arianna since the day she was born. If you think of her as my sister you will have the true picture.'

'That's it?' It was actually a lot more than she had expected him to tell her, and enough to set her pulse rate racing.

'That's all you're getting. Would you like some?'

'Some what?' Lisa froze, still debating the implications of a single and unattached Tino as he leaned towards her.

'Almonds and raisins.'

'Oh, yes...thank you.'

He filled their beakers with more wine.

The little she had learned about him had fuelled her curiosity, as well as her determination to keep his revelations on a roll. 'Tell me about that beautiful piano you have at Villa Aphrodite.'

On the point of handing her the beaker, he drew back. 'What do you want to know about it?'

'Do you play?'

'Yes.'

'Just "yes"?'

He shrugged. 'What more is there to know?'

She guessed he had already given her more information than he had ever given to anyone outside his inner circle, but that wasn't going to deter her from discovering more. Taking the beaker of wine from him, she said casually, 'I don't mean to probe, but—'

'If I need a private investigator,' Tino cut across her, 'I'll know who to call.'

'So you do enjoy playing the piano.'

Throwing back his head, he made a throaty, frustrated sound. 'Yes. Is that all?'

'If you'd rather not talk about it…'

'Oh, no,' he assured her sarcastically. 'I love to chat.'

'I gathered.'

'I learned to play the piano as an adult.'

Lisa went very still. 'You must be very good,' she said carefully, not wanting to push him too hard. 'Those are difficult, demanding pieces.'

'I play well enough.'

'I guess you needed a hobby.'

'You guess? Are you waiting for me to confirm or deny your guess, Lisa?'

'No, of course not—I'm sorry.'

'I always wanted to play the piano, that is all.'

'And you couldn't have lessons as a child?'

'No.' Impatience was pinging off him now. 'I couldn't have piano lessons until I paid for them myself.'

Lisa knew she was by no means the only child who had

yearned for things she couldn't have until the day she took charge of her own destiny, but something about Tino's stilted confession suggested he had wounds that ran deep. His lack of history intrigued her. Had he erased the past to hide something so terrible that even she could not imagine what it was? The thought that they might share something so intrinsic to their make-up was deeply unwelcome. It gave them a bond—a bond she didn't want to share with a man who held her company's fate in his hands; no one knew better than she how ruthless the past could make you.

'I first met Stella when I was a very small boy. She had an old piano and I loved the sound of it.'

Lifting up her head, Lisa hid her amazement. Tino had started talking about the past again, and without any prompting this time.

'Arianna was born when I was seven.'

'So, you grew up in the same neighbourhood?' *Damn, damn, damn!* Why couldn't she just learn to keep her mouth shut?

'Something like that. Shall we pack up?'

He had changed like quicksilver, and she knew that was the end of his revelations. She knew it because she recognised the same technique she always used to put up a smokescreen to hide the past. She would get nowhere pushing him now.

They travelled back with only the rhythm of the engine and the sibilance of the water streaming past the wooden boat breaking the stillness of late afternoon. Lisa could understand why Tino loved island life, and why he worked so hard to preserve his anonymity. To be able to exchange the feverish pace of the business world for the solitude of Stellamaris had to be the most precious thing he had... But still his past intrigued her. Why was it all such a secret? He had told her a little about the piano, and something about Stella and Arianna, but what else was he hiding?

Would she find out more on Stellamaris? Or would she leave the island knowing as little about Tino Zagorakis as she did now?

Glancing at him, Lisa realised that Stella was right: the Greeks did have a natural affinity with the sea. Had Tino named the island after his elderly friend? Or had Stella's parents chosen her name in tribute to their beautiful island home?

'Have you thought about dinner, Lisa?'

'Dinner?' It was the last thing on her mind. Tino had just cut the engine, and they were drifting slowly towards the mooring. She had been focused on the picturesque houses circling the quay—their Technicolor shades seemed to have been intensified by the fading light. 'I hadn't really thought about dinner. I suppose I'll eat later, on my balcony.'

'It would be a good opportunity to talk.'

'To talk?' Her heart started thundering. 'About business?'

'Of course.'

He sounded mildly impatient—and had every right to, Lisa realised. He would hardly welcome any further investigation into his life—and there was no question of them making small talk, since neither one of them was good at that.

'Well?' He was still staring at her.

'*Oy, Tino! Opa! Siga…Siga!*'

Hearing the warning shout, they both whipped around in time to see one of the local men gesticulating furiously.

'*Theos!*' Tino swung the wheel violently, narrowly avoiding a collision.

'That was close.' Lisa was still shaking with shock, but Tino had made the adjustment in time, and the fishing vessel slid neatly, if narrowly, into its berth beside the

Stellamaris Odyssey. 'I imagine that might have been an expensive mistake if you had crashed into your yacht.'

'Expensive mistake?' Tino stared at her for a moment, as if he couldn't quite believe what had happened, and then he stalked away to toss the mooring ropes to the man waiting on shore.

Straddling the deck and the shore, he looked magnificent. As the two men secured the ropes she could see how much bigger he was than the other man, but, even so, their movements were perfectly synchronised. It was as if they shared the same internal rhythm. If she had learned nothing more than this, Stellamaris was Tino's true home. But if that was so, then what drove him? What demon in Tino's past would make him leave his beautiful island home in search of new worlds to conquer, new deals to make?

She was sure now that they shared something more fundamental than business, and it was something very few people would have recognised. They both kept the past hidden, and though she didn't know what had happened to Tino yet she did know that the past had shaped them, made them both strong—but it was their weakness too.

CHAPTER SIX

ON THE walk back from the harbour Tino was lost in his own thoughts, giving Lisa all the space she needed to scroll through the events of an incredible day. Her lips were still burning from his kiss, and how was she supposed to forget that he had almost spanked her, or how aroused that had made her? What might have happened if he hadn't drawn back? Would she have lost control? Just thinking about all the possibilities was enough to excite her.

'I'll leave you now.'

Her cheeks reddened guiltily as he reclaimed her attention.

'I have to take the lobsters to Stella.' Reaching past her, he opened the garden gate.

He seemed to have forgotten the dinner invitation. 'I'll see you tomorrow morning at eight?' She spoke briskly. And when he didn't answer, she added, 'I can't let you win this by default because you never found time to listen to my proposal.'

'I don't need that kind of advantage, Lisa.'

'Let's wait until tomorrow before you get too confident?'

Tipping his head, he gave her one of his rare smiles. 'I'm looking forward to it.'

'In that case, I'll say goodnight.'

As she walked away Lisa hoped crazily that he would call her back. Almost immediately, she found she missed him... She missed walking with him, relaxing with him, talking to him... She missed everything about him—which was ridiculous. They had shared one day. But sharing was something she never did. The lack of privacy in the commune had seen to that. There had been no private space, no personal possessions. Her time there had made her self-ish. She knew that. Today had been different. Today she had experienced an alternative, and found she liked it. She liked it a lot.

Opening the door to her bedroom, Lisa smiled, remembering the moment Tino had almost crashed into the harbour wall. He hadn't come out of the day unscathed either. They had both been equally distracted. Tossing her battered sunhat on the bed, she freed her hair and ran her fingers through the tangles. She would take a long, lazy bath, and forget about dangerous Greek men—she had to focus on business now.

It was a very different bathroom from the sophisticated wet room she used at the apartment. In that ultra-modern space, minimalism ruled. Tino's preferred style was traditional, as if he appreciated the history behind every object. The various jars and crystal vases were exquisite, as was the beautiful pale peach fabric covering the antique chaise longue in one corner of the room. Everything had been chosen with care, or maybe he had inherited the lot from his wealthy parents...

The commune had been littered with other people's junk. All she craved now in her life were a few highly sought after examples of modern craftsmanship—precious items, carefully selected, and then kept like museum pieces for her pleasure alone, almost as if she needed to remind herself that no one could force her to share them.

When she walked onto the balcony after her bath she was forced to dodge out of sight, seeing Tino deep in conversation with one of his gardeners. It had been foolish to walk outside wrapped in nothing but a towel, but the sunset had drawn her. The remarkable light had bathed the two men in an other-worldly glow, and even the petals of the flowers they were holding seemed lit by some spectral fire.

Then she remembered the taxi driver telling her that the May Day festivities required every house on Stellamaris to be filled with flowers. The meeting between Tino and his gardener would be something to do with that, she supposed. The gardener was probably outlining his plans, while Tino was making his selection from the available blooms.

The May Day celebrations would start on Friday. Had Tino planned this week knowing he would be too wrapped up in local festivities to spare time for their business discussions?

On this point at least, Lisa felt confident. Tino Zagorakis would never forego the chance of a business deal in favour of a local flower festival.

She would have to put her suit back on, Lisa realised, returning inside—or the trousers and shirt part of it, at least. She hadn't brought anything more with her than her swimming things, a change of underwear and tops, and her pyjamas. She had not expected to be staying longer than a couple of nights at most...

As she opened the wardrobe door Lisa exclaimed with surprise. It certainly wasn't empty now. Her initial thought was that all the beautiful outfits must belong to Arianna, but as she ran her hand along the rail she could see that they still had labels attached, as if they had been sent on approval from some high-class boutique.

She frowned, and pulled back. Was this Tino's idea? If they were meant for her, she couldn't accept them. Of course she couldn't accept them. But on the other hand, if she was staying until Friday she had to have something to wear. And she already had to pay him back for the sunhat and cream—she could just add this to the tally...

A quick call to the housekeeper confirmed they were for her. Tino had judged her dress size accurately, suggesting he had made some pretty thorough observations. Lisa felt heat flood through her, and then as she remembered the chest of drawers across the room excitement rushed through her. Nothing like this had ever happened to her.. and, surely, there couldn't be anything else?

Wrapping her fingers around the handles, she dragged a drawer open and stared inside. A sigh slowly peeled out of her. Underwear that she had only ever lusted after before was stacked—not laid, but stacked in neat piles—and arranged carefully according to colour. Of course she could easily have afforded any of it, but where clothes were concerned she was frugal. In the commune dozens of outfits had been shared around, but she had always worn the same threadbare track suit, guarding it jealously. The habit had stuck; though her clothes were no longer threadbare, she still kept her wardrobe to a minimum.

On the rare occasions when her father had pressed money into her hands so she didn't disgrace herself at a social function, she had spent as little as possible, returning the change to a man who had been as bemused by his daughter's parsimony as he had been appalled by her mother's reckless transfer of funds to the commune. Treating herself had been out of the question, wasting her father's money unthinkable, and she still kept rigid control of her finances. This abundance of luxury goods was like every birthday come at once...

It certainly beat having things sent on approval to the office, Lisa reflected ruefully as she rummaged through the drawer. Who, for goodness' sake, had time to choose briefs made of the finest flesh-coloured gossamer net? As she held them up she knew that her decision to keep some of the things was already made. She might be destined to eat dinner alone, but she was going to be dressed to kill.

She chose an elegant floor-length silk skirt in dove-grey with a matching camisole that had a toning, chiffon overshirt in shades of grey and smoky lilac. The colours were ideal for her complexion, and she wore her hair down. In one of the drawers she was stunned to find a pair of beautiful amethyst earrings in a small velvet case. She never wore jewellery, but these were gorgeous—and whoever had chosen them had exquisite taste. Maybe she would develop a taste for jewellery too, Lisa mused, viewing her reflection in the floor-length mirror.

She turned at a knock on the door, feeling rather foolish as she hurried to open it. She was dressed for an occasion, not to eat dinner alone on her balcony.

'Oh.' Lisa stared with amazement at the vast floral arrangement the maid was holding out to her.

'For you, Thespinis Bond.'

'Are you sure?'

The girl looked at her.

Of course, she was sure, Lisa realised, kicking her sluggish brain cells into action as she stood back to let the young girl into the room.

'Shall I put them over here for you, Thespinis Bond, where you can see them from the bed?' The maid hovered by an ornate console table.

'Yes, please. That's definitely the right place for them... They're magnificent.'

'They are all from the gardens here at Villa Aphrodite.'

'Oh.'

'I almost forgot, Thespinis Bond. There is a card for you.'

Taking the vellum envelope, Lisa waited until the maid had left the room before opening it. Her heart started to thump heavily as she read the firm, uncompromising script. 'I would be delighted if you could join me for dinner this evening, Tino.'

So he hadn't forgotten. Her heart was hammering like a piston. She was excited and apprehensive too. A small part of her wanted this to be the most romantic thing that had ever happened to her—that was ever likely to happen to her—but she knew she had to be wary of Tino's motives. This was all very nice, but she couldn't afford to be distracted yet again from the purpose of her visit. Was this just part of his business plan—his well-thought-out strategy to soften her up? Everyone said Tino Zagorakis would stop at nothing. Was this just another example of the tactics he was prepared to employ?

As Lisa stared at the beautiful flowers they might as well have sprouted darts all aimed in her direction. There was another discreet tap on the door, and when she opened it Lisa found the same maid hovering.

'I'm sorry to trouble you again, Thespinis Bond, but Kirie Zagorakis would like your answer now. Will you be joining him for dinner, or would you prefer to dine in your room tonight?'

'Tell him...' Lisa glanced towards the balcony where she could see the lights from the garden reflected on the stone balustrade. Whatever Tino's motives, she didn't feel like hiding in her room. 'Tell him I will be down shortly.'

She couldn't delay any longer, Lisa realized, laying her hairbrush on the dressing table. She had brushed her hair so vigorously and for so long it was springing out around her shoulders. A spritz of perfume, and a slick of lip-gloss, and she was ready...

Tino turned the moment she walked onto the balcony. It was almost as if he could sense her presence before he saw her.

'You look beautiful.'

'Thank you. You look different too,' Lisa observed dryly.

'Yes, well, I thought I might as well make an effort,' he said casually.

As they stared at each other Lisa found she was smiling. But she had to keep part of herself aloof if she was ever to stand a chance of remaining immune to Tino. He was wearing a black dinner suit that made him look more handsome than ever—if such a thing was possible. The white, open-necked shirt was a startling contrast against his tanned skin—and she was blatantly staring at him, Lisa realised, quickly looking away.

She was so beautiful it was the easiest thing in the world to forget about business. And business was the purpose of every moment he spent with her. It was easy to forget about dinner too, and just take her to bed...

He had never felt such unbridled lust for any woman. And why should he hold back when there was no reason to do so? Time was running out, after all. And she was smiling at him—and looking as if she meant it. He was getting the hang of this wooing business. Just as he had expected, the day out on the fishing smack had thrown all her preconceptions about him into confusion. The clothes that had been flown in for her from the top Athenian designers had clearly delighted her, or she wouldn't be wearing them. The modest jewellery was a masterstroke—the amethyst earrings gleamed in the candlelight, setting off her sun-kissed skin, drawing his eye to the lustre of her hair, and making her even more beautiful for him. Next time he'd buy her emeralds to bring out the colour of her eyes.

They couldn't stand like this staring at each other for ever, Lisa realised, still smiling as she walked forward. She felt strangely bashful, but then she wasn't used to presenting herself for a man's approval. And, for some reason, what Tino thought about her appearance really did matter to her.

'You look lovely, Lisa.' Taking hold of her hand, he raised it to his lips.

At his touch a quiver ran through her, and it didn't stop there, so she pulled her hand away—too late.

He searched her face.

She stared at him and heard a little cry, and then realised that it was her own voice and that Tino had swung her into his arms.

As he strode inside the house with her all the servants seemed to have disappeared. He mounted the stairs swiftly, holding her close and safe in his arms. When they reached the top landing he shifted her weight effortlessly, and opened a door. Walking inside, he kicked it shut behind them, and lowered her to the ground in front of him, steadying her on her feet.

Gazing up, Lisa thought she saw something in Tino's eyes that mirrored her own need. Acting on impulse, she reached up and wrapped her arms around his neck. Pulling back, he stared down at her for a few moments, as if he had to confirm something.

Lisa wasn't sure which of them moved first, which of them gave in first. She only knew that she needed to feel Tino pressed up hard against her. She needed his mouth to claim hers with the same urgency she had to draw her next breath. And then they were kissing each other passionately, and she had her fingers laced through his hair, keeping him fast, pressing against him with all the hunger a lifetime of denial could produce. She heard the sounds of passion she was making, and didn't care. Nothing mattered now—all she cared about was that Tino didn't let her go, and that this time he didn't leave her unsatisfied, because now she wanted all of him, with no restrictions, no boundaries, no doubts...

They were like two lions mating, raw, primitive, desperate, hungry. There was so much sex in the air it formed a miasma around them, invading their nostrils, and sending them both hurtling off to a place where no clear thought was possible, and only sensation and hunger existed; hunger that only one act could relieve.

'I need you,' Lisa gasped as Tino lifted her into his arms.

'*Thee mou!* I need you more,' he ground out as he carried her over to the bed.

'No—don't rip it off.' She closed her hands protectively over the chiffon over-blouse, suddenly nervous, suddenly conscious of what they were about to do.

'I'll buy you another, *Thespinis mou.*'

'But I like this one.'

'Then take it off,' he instructed roughly. 'Take it off for me, *yineka mou.*'

She was panting, eyes wide. She was his equal and that made her feel safe. Slipping off the bed, Lisa undid the sash at the front and then allowed the chiffon blouse to fall. As it floated to the floor she felt no fear. There was an unspoken connection between them that for some reason made her trust him. Watching Tino take her place on the bed and then stretch out like a sleek black panther was more seduction than she could take.

'Continue,' he instructed lazily.

'No.' She stared fiercely at him. 'This is far too one-sided.'

Quirking a brow, he sat up and shrugged off his jacket.

'Get rid of it.' She could see he was as aroused as she was, and then he indicated that it was her turn now.

Slowly easing the straps of the silk camisole from her shoulders, Lisa let it drop. Then, swooping down, she took it from the floor by one finger. She was wearing nothing underneath.

'Have you no shame?' Tino murmured appreciatively.

'None.' Gazing down, Lisa saw how taut her nipples had become. They seemed to be stretching out to him to both tease and provoke his censure. Raising her head, she gazed steadily into his eyes.

'Just as I'd hoped.' He quickly opened the buttons on his shirt.

'Take it off.' Her voice was firm, and once he had

obeyed her she rewarded him, arching her back and displaying her breasts to their best advantage.

Easing back on the pillows, she noted the thrust of his arousal.

'Have *you* no shame?' she demanded softly, her voice thick with desire.

Stroking down the length of it, he looked at her. 'None…would you like me to develop some?'

'It's a little late for that, I should imagine.' Lisa found her hands were shaking as she reached for the fastening on her skirt. 'And I'll be sure to make you pay if you do.'

'I'm counting on it.'

Slipping her finger down beneath the waistband, Lisa closed her eyes as she allowed the column of silk to pool at her feet.

'And now the rest,' Tino insisted, referring to the transparent pants she was wearing.

Lisa shook her head. 'It's your turn now—'

'Who is going to make me?'

'Me.' It came out on a breath, but she couldn't move; she was transfixed by his lips, lips she wanted to feel all over her body, possessing her mouth, possessing her totally, utterly, everywhere…

Lying back on the bed, Tino caught hold of the brass rail behind his head and stretched out.

Taking her cue, Lisa picked up the chiffon over-blouse and walked to the head of the bed.

'What are you going to do with that?'

'I'm going to tie you down, and then do whatever I want with you—'

'I don't think so.'

It happened so fast. One minute she was standing there, and the next she was flat on her back on the bed staring into eyes that were blazing with desire.

'I had to save you from yourself,' Tino explained softly,

making a pretence of contrition. 'I knew how precious the top was to you. How could I let you use it to tie me up?'

Lisa gasped and writhed beneath him as he began teasing her ear lobe with his teeth. 'I'm guessing you'd buy me another?' Her words came out in a hectic whisper.

'And so I will,' he assured her. 'I'll buy you a thousand tops if you want them, but I'll never let you master me, Lisa Bond.'

'Is the missionary position all I'm good for, then?' Her lips curved with amusement as she stared into his eyes.

'Pleasure is what you're good for. But pleasure on my terms, not yours.'

Somehow she managed to slip away. 'Then there can be no pleasure for either of us.'

Reaching out, he caught her back to him. 'I decide about the levels of pleasure in this relationship.'

'Oh, you do?'

'Just answer one question. Do you want me?'

'Yes, I want you...' Lisa hesitated, and then admitted softly, 'I want you more than anything.'

Tino fought the feeling rising in his chest. This had nothing to do with emotion. He just wanted to give her more pleasure than she had ever known, pleasure she would remember for the rest of her life, pleasure that would make every other man fall short in her eyes... He concentrated his attention on the tiny pants she was wearing. He pressed his palm against her stomach and felt her quiver of desire course up his arm. She was trembling with passion and so he slipped his fingers beneath the waistband to tease her.

'Don't stop, Tino.'

She writhed beneath him. 'What are you asking me to do, Lisa? You have to tell me exactly what you want—or how can I possibly know?'

'You know what I want you to do,' she told him fiercely.

'But I have to hear it from your mouth.' He rubbed the

thumb pad of one hand roughly over the full swell of her bottom lip.

'I want you to…'

'Yes? You want me to do what to you, Lisa? You have to tell me.'

'I'm… ' She hesitated, and then she saw the change in his eyes. He was so intuitive she didn't have to explain a thing.

'You're a virgin?' He turned suddenly serious.

'Not exactly. I've just never—' She blushed red.

'What does ''not exactly'' mean, Lisa? You either are or you aren't a virgin. It's one of life's few absolutes.'

'I've never had sex with a man.'

'That's not so bad, is it?' Cupping her chin, he turned her to face him so she couldn't evade his stare.

'It's not that simple. I've never had time for relationships. But back at my apartment, I have a drawer full of—'

'Please—I really don't need to hear the details.' And now he smiled wickedly. 'If I do, you may convince me that all the rumours I hear are true.'

'What rumours are those?' Lisa was immediately defensive.

'That women may very soon be able to do without men altogether?'

'Why don't I believe you?' She smiled, relaxing again as he tried for a crestfallen expression.

'You don't believe I have insecurities?'

She raised a brow.

'You'd be surprised.'

'I certainly would.'

He couldn't play games any longer. He couldn't wait any longer. He had never felt like this before. Dragging her to him, he turned her, and had her beneath him in the space of a few seconds. He kissed her until he could feel her arching against him. He brought her on top of him then, so that he could cup her bottom and stroke her the way he was very sure she would like.

She sighed raggedly. 'You have to stop that.'

'Why?'

'Because it feels so good.'

'Then that's the only encouragement I need to continue.'

She whimpered with pleasure, helpless beneath his touch, relishing the way he was massaging her buttocks and, in the process, pressing her hard against his rigid erection. 'That feels so good.' A shudder of pure lust consumed Lisa's body as she stared into Tino's eyes. 'I'd like to—'

'Like to what?'

'Continue.' She smiled against his mouth.

'In that case…' Catching hold of her wrists, he turned her again, pinning her securely beneath him.

She had never done this with anyone. She had never trusted anyone enough. With Tino it was different, because she didn't feel frightened of him…and that was because when Tino touched her, even when he held her pinned down like this, she knew he would never forget himself, he would never forget how vulnerable she was pitting her strength against his. He knew how firmly to hold her, and when to let go. He could read every nuance in her face, and had mastered his prodigious strength so she could wrestle with him and still feel safe.

The warmth in her heart was threatening to overwhelm her, Lisa realised, feeling her eyes fill with tears. Fire was rushing through her limbs at the thought of making love with him, but there was something even more compelling building inside her… Was it tenderness? *Or could it be love?* It was something she had never felt before, so it was hard to be sure—and then Tino greedily seized one of her tightly extended nipples and began to suckle, and no more thoughts were possible…

Lisa cried out with delighted surprise, lacing her fingers

through his hair to urge him on. Why hadn't she known pleasure like this existed? Why had she never felt this way before? When Tino stopped briefly to read her face she made an angry sound, and kept on making it until he found the other nipple and suckled on that one too.

'That's better,' she approved throatily. 'I like that.'

'Oh, do you?' He lifted himself on one elbow to stare into her face. 'And do I exist solely for your pleasure now?'

She considered his question through narrowed eyes. 'I don't see why not.'

As she gazed at him he could feel her strength and her certainty. They were worthy combatants. 'Then don't you think you should take these off?'

'Let me,' she insisted, and he watched as she ripped off the fragile briefs. Her boldness excited him. The fragile briefs were as much a hindrance to her as they were to him. This was a joust between equals; each of them wanted to see how far the other would push. 'Lie down,' he murmured, aching to pleasure her. 'Lie down, and spread your legs.'

She was clearly shocked by his suggestion—but her eyes were brighter than ever, and her cheeks were flushed pink with excitement. He trailed his fingers very lightly between her legs to feel how wet she was. Closing her eyes, she groaned, and then opened them a little wider for him. When he stopped, her eyes flashed open.

'That's not fair.'

'What isn't fair?' He pulled back to look at her.

'You sound so stern.' She seemed pleased by it. Turning onto her side, she rested her chin on her elbow to stare up at him. 'You *are* stern,' she observed huskily. 'Mmm, I like that.'

'Do you?' His senses roared as he caught her meaning.

'Yes, I do.'

As she reached for his trousers he caught hold of her

wrist, stopping her. 'You're a very naughty girl, aren't you, Lisa?'

'If I'm naughty, will you punish me?' she responded teasingly.

His breath caught in his throat as she stared at him. When she looked at him like that he longed to put her over his knee just as he had on the cliff path, but this time he wouldn't stop… This time he would give her exactly what she wanted. He could see she was remembering what had almost happened there, and that it was exciting her as much as it was exciting him.

He couldn't believe what she was asking him to do; he couldn't believe how much he wanted to do it. The thought of attending to those impudent curves made his throat tighten with anticipation. She had an extremely narrow waist that emphasised the fullness of her hips, and from his vantage point her bottom appeared to be a perfect pink globe…palest pink. She was thrusting it towards him now as he stared at her, almost as if she could read his mind…and now she was writhing a little to tempt him still more. 'Are you asking me to put you over my knee?'

'Would you?'

She made it sound more like a request, than a question. 'Do you want me to, you naughty girl?'

'Maybe—if you can catch me.'

'What?'

'You don't seriously expect me to mildly submit, do you, Tino?'

'I'm not sure.' His senses flared. She was inviting him to indulge in a tussle they both knew could only have one conclusion.

'Naughty girls don't just roll over and submit.'

'Don't they?' He gave her a firm look.

'No…they're rebellious, and cunning, and—'

She shrieked as he caught hold of her, and then they

rolled over once, twice…and then they were falling… falling off the bed.

She was laughing, he saw with relief. 'Are you all right?'

'I will be soon,' she promised provocatively. 'I suppose I should be grateful that you brought me on top of you to cushion my fall… I suppose I should be relieved that your reflexes are so sharp.'

Everything was a tease now. She had moved away from him, and she was on her hands and knees, staring at him like a beautiful pussy-cat, her eyes narrowed to arrow slits of emerald. Her bottom was raised high, displayed to its best advantage. He relished the moment, sure she couldn't possibly know the effect the sight of it was having on him…but then she undulated, and even raised it a little higher, proving that she knew exactly what she was doing.

'You *are* a bad girl,' he observed huskily.

'Tino… I want it.'

She gasped as he moved quickly behind her. Kneeling on the floor, he stroked his hands lightly over her naked rump. 'Down,' he said softly.

She obeyed him at once, resting her head on her arms so that her bottom was raised as high as it could be. He dealt her several firm strokes, and had the satisfaction of hearing her call throatily for more. The next few ended in a caress that brought her very close and that was his cue to lift her to her feet. Holding her in front of him with their faces almost touching, he very slowly stroked his hands up her arms relishing the sight of the shudders coursing through her. 'I had no idea this was going to turn out to be quite so energetic, or half so dangerous.'

'Are you frightened of me, Tino?' She whispered the words against his mouth.

Even he didn't know the truth to that. She made him feel things he shouldn't be feeling… She unsettled him more than any woman he had ever known… She pushed him further than he had ever considered going with a woman before. 'More to the point,' he said, 'are you frightened of me?' He searched her eyes.

'I'm in more danger from this.'

'Oh,' he murmured softly as she cupped him through his evening trousers.

'I'm glad you understand me.'

'Oh, I do,' he assured her as he reached to undo his zip.

'Let me,' Lisa whispered.

He held his hands out to the side.

'That's better.' She held his gaze as she undressed him, and only broke it when she was forced to dip down to remove his trousers completely and toss them away. 'Now you get your reward.'

But as she reached for him he pulled away.

'Not before I give you yours.' He swept her up.

'If you insist.'

And he did…

CHAPTER SEVEN

LISA shrieked with shock and with excitement as Tino joined her. As he pulled her on top of him she dropped a kiss on his firm mouth. 'You're not going to get away from me now.'

'As I'd hoped,' he murmured. 'Shall we begin?'

'Oh, please,' she sighed, reaching for him. Now the barriers were down between them his clean male scent was all the aphrodisiac she needed. Yet still he played with her, holding her away from him, refusing her any satisfaction. Cupping her chin, he caressed the sensitive area just below her ear...but when she tried to kiss him on the mouth he made a sound of denial down low in his throat, and held her away again. She wriggled against him, wanting the touch of his hands, needing it desperately. 'You will send me crazy, teasing me like this,' she complained breathlessly.

'Not crazy, just into a deeper state of arousal,' he observed clinically.

'You sound so cold.' She laughed it off, confident that it was a figment of her imagination.

Pulling away, he lavished a look down the whole trembling length of her.

'Hold me, Tino. Touch me.'

Her words drove him. His passions had never been roused to such a level. But he must keep control...that way he would give her more pleasure than she had ever dreamed of.

'You're not making me wait any longer,' she insisted fiercely.

He caught her wrist as she reached for him, and held both her hands over her head, keeping them secure in one fist on the pillow. She didn't try to resist him. 'So, you've no more fight left in you?'

'I didn't say that—but if you use your strength there's no contest.'

He released her immediately, and she sprang to the other side of the bed, staring at him, teasing him…

'I'm a naughty girl, Tino…or had you forgotten?'

'I have not forgotten anything, Lisa.' Nor had he. He remembered Bond Steel, and how she had set herself against him. 'Before I give you what you want, you must welcome my authority.'

Seeing the change in Tino's eyes, Lisa shivered with desire. 'Can you master me?'

'Let me ask you a question, Lisa… Do you want me to pleasure you?'

'You know I do.'

'Then you must convince me that you will submit to my command.'

'Never.' The single word left her lips on a sigh…a sigh that was laced with all the temptation she could muster, and her expression tempted him on still more.

'Never?' he queried softly. 'Do you want your bottom smacking again, Lisa?'

Lisa could hardly breathe with excitement as she nodded suggestively. Her lips were moist as she gazed at him spellbound with fascination at the thought of what might lie in store for her.

She shrieked as he rolled her over his knees. The sudden impact of Tino's warm hand on her soft flesh was so good. Lisa shrieked again, and wriggled her buttocks to show her approval. The pressure of his hard thighs against her was electrifying, and he judged the spanking perfectly. She knew he meant to rouse her all the more, and he had succeeded.

His hand lingered, and his skilful fingers, warm and firm, curled around her buttocks until he nearly, so very nearly, touched her where she ached to be touched. Nothing had ever felt this good, but it still wasn't enough. 'How can you tease me like this?'

'Did I give you permission to question my actions, you naughty, naughty girl?'

With each word, Tino's hand landed firmly on the soft pink swell of Lisa's bottom until she thought she would pass out from an overdose of pleasure.

'Have you learned your lesson yet?' he demanded.

'No!' Lisa exclaimed as loud as she could when her face was muffled by the bedclothes and she was teetering on the edge of the biggest climax of her life. 'I need much more. Oh…' She sighed with pleasure as he changed his touch into a stroke.

She was moving now, rubbing herself against him, lifting her buttocks towards his hand, inviting more and more of the delicious taps. She was more aroused than she had ever been. She had needed this. It made her trust him, showed her how right it could be with the right man. She had to have him now—all of him. 'All right, all right—I submit…'

Swinging her round, Tino settled her on the soft bank of pillows. 'Say it, then.'

'Say what?'

'I, Lisa Bond…'

'I, Lisa Bond,' Lisa repeated huskily, holding his stare.

'Submit to whatever you decide will bring me most pleasure.'

'That's far too much for me to remember,' she complained, reaching for him.

'Submit,' he growled, dragging her close.

Lisa's eyes darkened as she looked at him. 'Not without a fight.'

'Of course. I would hate to disappoint you.'

And this time when Tino kissed her he denied her nothing. Just the touch of his warm, naked flesh pressing against her body drew whimpers of pleasure from her lips. His arms were strong and firm around her, and he kissed her passionately, tenderly, letting her show him what she wanted, and then responding with more skill than she could ever have imagined a man might be capable of.

'Oh, Tino, I love—'

He silenced her with another kiss, frightened of what she might say, frightened of the depth of feeling welling inside him. He wasn't supposed to feel anything outside the need to satisfy them both. He was in a hurry to lose himself in sensation and ease the pain that came with knowing he didn't deserve anything good...

'Tino?'

When she saw the expression in his eyes Lisa looked away. The emptiness was too much to bear. Looking into each other's eyes was like looking into a mirror. They were both so frightened of being hurt again, and they'd had more than enough pain as children to last them a lifetime. 'Will you make love to me now?'

He smiled slowly. She was the most desirable woman he had ever met, and she was prompting him? 'I've never had to be reminded of my duty before.'

'Your duty? And I don't want to hear about *before*.'

She was right. She was a virgin. It had to be special for her. He would make sure it was. 'I have to be sure this is what you want.'

'I am sure—and I don't think you need much prompting now.' She wrapped her hands around him.

The breath gusted out of his lungs at her touch. 'That feels so good.'

He had never taken a woman so carefully, so tenderly, or with such tightly reined in passion. Lisa's only experience had been at her own hands. He could understand it, it made perfect sense; she was always in control that way. It made him super-aware of her now, super-sensitive to her breathing, and to the look in her eyes, to the set of her mouth, and to the touch of her hands on his body. He wanted it to be perfect for her. He wanted it to be the first time that either of them had ever felt like this.

Lisa drew in a sharp breath as Tino entered her, and then softened when she felt his brief hesitation. She didn't want him to think he was hurting her and stop. The surprise at his size had been welcome, the panic over almost before it began. She had never imagined it could be like this, that any man could be so tender, that she could feel so cherished, or so safe. 'Please, Tino...please don't stop.'

Caressing her with his warm, strong hands, he did as she asked, tipping her up to meet him so that he could inhabit her completely, and then he groaned as she tightened her muscles around him, drawing him deeper still.

'Are you sure you want this?' He nuzzled her neck as she bucked beneath him.

'Yes, but more than anything I want to please you.'

'You are pleasing me,' he assured her.

He made his strokes deep and slow, relishing the sight of her passion-dampened face. He gave the greatest pleasure he could as the silken noose of her body sucked on him convulsively. He applied a little more pressure at the end of each long thrust until finally she gazed at him in disbelief.

'It's so good,' she managed breathlessly. 'Oh, please don't stop... Don't ever stop.'

Her fingernails raked across his shoulders. He barely felt the pain as he slowed the pace to keep her teetering above the abyss of intense sensation for as long as he could. But then the tension in her face, the absolute hunger in her eyes, as well as the apprehension he sensed in her as she approached pleasure beyond her understanding, proved too much for him, and with a few firm strokes he pushed her over the edge.

She cried out then, joyously, continuously, as if the powerful spasms would never end. He held her firmly and it took all his strength just to keep her in position without hurting her while he made sure that she didn't miss a single, satisfying moment of pleasure.

He calmed her afterwards with long, soothing strokes, until she stirred restlessly again. 'Aren't you satisfied yet?'

'I'll never have enough of you,' she admitted, knowing she meant that in every way.

'What else do you have in mind?'

As he teased her she drew back inwardly into her little shell of uncertainty. She wanted one thing, but Tino wanted something else. And she wanted too much. 'How about I ride you into submission?' The front she could always put in place to hide uncertainty in any given situation had really come into its own, Lisa realised, tossing her hair back provocatively.

'To the finish, if you please.'

'If you insist.'

'I do insist,' Tino assured her, swinging her on top of him.

She eased down on him slowly, and rubbed herself rhythmically against him. She was composed entirely of sensation...

'No,' he insisted softly, 'let me do that for you.'

She gasped and slumped inert as his searching fingers found her, and gently, skillfully, began to work. 'I won't be able to move a muscle if you don't stop doing that.'

'Then I shall have to stop,' he said, pretending regret, 'because I'm holding you to your promise.'

When he took his hand away she started to move again, taking him deep inside her. But then she teased him, pulling back, and making him wait—but he was having none of it, and caught her to him again. Lisa's spirit soared as Tino took control, and as their eyes met in that moment they were one. He touched her delicately, and persuasively, until she could only move convulsively in time to a rhythm of his choice until they climaxed violently together.

Sleeping in Tino's arms was almost the best part of all, Lisa realised. She had woken in the middle of the night, and now she traced the line of his lips with one finger. She gasped as he captured the tip in his mouth. 'I thought you were asleep.'

'Barely.' He narrowed his eyes to look at her. 'In fact, I need very little sleep.'

'That's good to hear.'

'Isn't it?' he said, moving behind her. He nestled close so that he could touch her while he thrust into her. He played her well, judging her responses so finely that she angled herself shamelessly, moving so that he could see everything he was doing to her in the low light seeping into the room from the lanterns outside.

'You're quite a woman,' he murmured later when they were lying twined around each other.

Lisa could only manage to mumble groggily and snuggle a little closer. She felt so safe, so content it was like returning home after an arduous journey…

'Do you know how special you are?' Tino whispered as he stroked Lisa's hair. Her breathing was so even he knew she was asleep. And it was as well she couldn't hear him saying words that would have misled them both—dangerous words…

Instinct warned him to pull back while there was still time. There was only one possible ending to this—and it was the same ending he had envisaged the day he'd walked into the Bond Steel boardroom. And she would hate him when he took the company from her…

Moonlight was streaming into the bedroom as Tino started up in bed wide awake. He had fallen asleep so deeply he could hardly believe the old nightmare had returned. Springing out of bed, he paced the floor. Halting by the window, he gazed out, seeing nothing.

How could a man admit to having nightmares? How could a man live with such images in his mind? Why wasn't his will strong enough to get rid of them?

Hearing Lisa stir, he quietly opened the doors leading onto the balcony and stepped outside. Planting his hands on the stone balustrade, he stared out towards the horizon. Stella was the closest thing he had to a friend, and even Stella Panayotakis didn't know all the things that had happened to him in the orphanage. It was better she never knew… And yet the past had made him the man he was today—it drove his every move. It had given him a private island, unimaginable wealth, and even worldwide respect—the only thing it could never give him was the capacity to love.

He glanced back inside the room where he could see Lisa's hair spread out across the pillow like a cloud. Her face, deep in sleep, was pale and trusting like a child's in the moonlight… His appetite to compete with her, to subdue her in every way, had deserted him utterly. If he had been capable of love, he would have loved Lisa Bond. But learning to love, like learning to feel, was a luxury he could never buy. And more importantly he had embarked upon a journey that no one else could share…a lifelong journey that demanded everything of him, a journey that drove him from deal to deal in the endless quest for money to fund his dream, to sustain his project…

It shamed him that he had set out to triumph over her.

Taking Bond Steel from Lisa was one victory he didn't need…but there was something he could do to salve his conscience. He would buy her small engineering works. He would give her the break she so desperately needed… He would give a little, just this once. She deserved that much—as that was all he could give. He would send the necessary information right away.

He would have liked to do more for her, but anything on a personal level was out of his reach. Straightening up, Tino stretched out his powerful limbs and turned his face up to the stars. He was a man people envied, a man who could buy anything he desired, but he was a man with nothing, because he had nothing to give. He had nothing to offer Lisa other than money and sex—and she deserved someone better than that. Someone better than him.

Lisa woke to another beautiful day. But then every day was more beautiful than the last on Stellamaris. Stretching languorously in Tino's bed, she felt the empty space at her side and looked around for him. The room was empty. He would be swimming, she remembered, sighing deeply with contentment.

Propping herself up on the soft bank of pillows, she viewed the spacious room with interest. A mischievous smile curved her lips. She hadn't taken it all in the previous night, because Tino had demanded all her attention.

It was much as she might have expected: a man's space—marble floors, state-of-the-art sound centre, plain walls, neutral colours, and a couple of extraordinary pieces of modern art on the walls. Hockney, Lisa realised as she identified the vibrant images created by the British artist from Bradford.

Tino's room. Smiling to herself, Lisa snuggled back on the pillows. She had never felt like this before… She had been waiting for Tino Zagorakis all her life. Even when she closed the biggest deal, or when she remembered the day her father had handed over the reins of Bond Steel to her—nothing, *nothing* came close to the way she was feeling now, after spending the night in Tino's arms.

She had felt safe in his arms…*in a man's arms*. She had felt cherished for the first time in her life. She had felt Tino's arms around her, sometimes seeking nothing more than an affectionate hug, which had meant more to her than she could safely express without breaking down and spoiling the day with ugly comparisons.

She had never known affection; she had never known how wonderful a touch, a gesture, or just a simple look from someone who really cared for you could be. And then Tino had made love to her…really made love to her. So he really did love her a little bit, even if expressing his emotions didn't come easily to him.

And what a lover. Lisa eased her body on the bed, feeling all the unaccustomed signs of lengthy lovemaking… But they'd had fun too. She had never in her wildest dreams imagined that sex could be such fun. And they had laughed together, as much as they had desired each other, and felt a ravening hunger for each other. They had laughed together…

She laughed now, dashing away tears of sheer emotion. She had never thought of herself as an emotional person before; she'd spent all of her life hiding her emotions, pretending they didn't exist. But one night with Tino had reduced her to an emotional mess. What she felt for him was so wonderful, so unexpected, such a revelation, she didn't have a clue how she was going to handle all the feelings competing for space inside her.

Leaping out of bed, she hunted for his bathroom. Doors, doors: closets, dressing-rooms—one with nothing but casual shirts and jeans, another with suits at one end, and those see-through-fronted drawers at the other, holding goodness knew what. She was laughing again by the time she found the bathroom. As she might have expected, it was fabulous. Clad in black marble, the shower alone was big enough for a rugby team! She wouldn't waste time on a bath, though that was easily big enough for two... She had seen baths like it in magazines, but even in her own rather splendid bathroom at the villa there was nothing approaching this scale of opulence. Once she was showered, and dressed casually in cream cotton trousers and a sky-blue short-sleeved shirt, she knew exactly what she wanted to do...

What this room needs is a woman's touch, Lisa reflected as she turned full circle still fixing her hair in a casual ponytail. Flowers...flowers like the ones Tino had sent to her room, only even better than those... She would go downstairs and seek the gardener's help.

The kitchen was busy when she found the same young girl who had brought the flowers up to her room. Fortunately, Maria spotted her, and came across at once to see if she could be of help.

'These flowers are for Kirie Zagorakis,' Lisa explained, 'Could you help me with them, Maria? Do you have a vase?'

'*Malista*—of course, Thespinis Bond.' Maria glanced back to where her colleagues were hurrying about.

Lisa thought the young girl looked a little anxious. 'It seems very busy in here. Are you sure I won't get you into trouble?'

'No, I am happy to help you,' Maria assured her. 'Come over here, Thespinis Bond. You can arrange them at the sink we use for such things.'

The flowers were magnificent. Lisa had chosen them to complement the reds, orange, green and pinks of the Hockney painting. Gazing round Tino's room, she decided to set them on a low Swedish-style table opposite the picture.

Standing back to admire her handiwork, she sighed. 'Perfect.' Now all she had to do was to find Tino and spring the surprise on him. Why shouldn't men have romantic gestures made to them? She could already picture them, arms linked as she dragged him along, teasing him… He would pretend to hold back… He would be puzzled, but laughing—they would both laugh. She couldn't wait to see his face when she brought him back to his room…

Tino frowned as he cut the line. Lisa wasn't in her room. No one in the house seemed to know where she had gone. He should have woken her…but she had looked so peaceful. She would be down on the beach, he guessed, and if so it would be hours before she returned…

He rang the housekeeper, and asked her to send someone down to the beach to find Thespinis Bond for him. The kitchen was in uproar, he could hear all the hectic preparations in the background. It pleased him to know that his household was equal to any task he set them. He ran a tight ship, a successful ship; everything on Stellamaris ran like clockwork…

CHAPTER EIGHT

'LISA—'

Lisa blenched as Tino sprang to his feet.

She felt sick…sick and stupid all at once. It wasn't a feeling that crept up on her as she gazed around the room Maria had directed her to; it hit her straight in the stomach like a blow.

The men gathered around the boardroom table were all in business suits—lightweight, but formal nonetheless. Tino, of course, was dressed casually, but in his own particular style that denoted rank as well as authority. His jeans were expensive, his shirt beautifully tailored, and as always he was immaculately groomed. His thick, wavy black hair—the same glossy black hair she had laced her fingers through, moulding the scalp beneath with an urgency approaching frenzy when he had made love to her; *that hair*— was swept back from his handsome brow and was still slightly damp, as if he had only just emerged from the shower after his swim…

Everyone was staring at her…and these were hard-bitten men, her men, along with Tino's board of directors—chosen for their business acumen, not for their compassion. She was horribly exposed—without make-up, her hair casually arranged, her feet bare, her clothes simple.

To Tino's credit, he came around the table to her at once. 'Excuse us, gentlemen. I will be back with you shortly.'

Guiding her out, he closed the door behind them quietly and leaned back against it, as if to ensure they could not be followed.

Lisa managed, 'I didn't realise—' before Tino shut his
eyes, as if he accepted part of the blame…as if she should
have known, as if the moment she had walked into the
room had been as agonising for him as it had been for her.

'No one could find you. Where the hell were you?'

'In the garden.' Her voice was shaking. 'In the kitchen,
and then back in your room.'

'They must have missed you. I tried to find you, Lisa,
to warn you I'd set up an emergency meeting—I sent people to find you.'

'I don't understand… What's everyone doing here?'

'You wanted this deal so badly…I thought if I brought
everyone over—' He stopped and looked at a point somewhere over her head. 'I wanted to give you the best chance.
My people have identified a better deal with Clifton—but
you already know that.'

'Tino?' Her voice sounded small, and wounded, and Lisa
hated herself for the weakness, but she wasn't in charge of
her body now, or her powers of speech.

'You'd better go and get changed—'

Tino sounded so cool, so businesslike, so logical…so
distant…

'I will call for coffee—it will distract them,' he said, as
if he was thinking out loud. 'By the time you return, they
will have forgotten. When you come back, they will have
forgotten what they saw, and think only of business, of the
money to be made.'

There was nothing in his eyes for her, Lisa realised.
Nothing. Even now that he was looking straight at her, there
was nothing there, nothing at all… She might have imagined what had happened between them the previous night
for all the recognition there was in that stare. It was back
to business. 'You're quite sure of all this, are you, Tino?'
she said coldly. 'You're quite sure they will have forgotten
what a fool I just made of myself?' She hardened her

mouth, her face, her mind, and her heart, kicking herself back into cold, emotion-free business mode. Jack Bond was right, after all—there was no room for emotion in business.

'I'll be back in exactly a quarter of an hour,' she said briskly when Tino didn't say a word. 'I'll want to start the meeting promptly, so see the coffee is cleared away by then.'

Lisa spent the rest of that day with her head buried in figures, balance sheets and predictions. She had never welcomed them more.

Tino was right about one thing: there had been a brief tension when she'd walked back into the room. But once she was safely dressed in business armour—sharp suit, crisp white blouse, heels clacking in a steady, reassuring rhythm across the marble floor—her confidence had quickly been restored. Everyone could see that everything was back to normal: her hair neatly dressed in its customary chignon, her lips carefully outlined in peach, her make-up applied with a steady hand... Only her heart was in pieces, and that was the one thing no one could see.

Lisa had her head bent over the document under discussion and was almost caught out when everyone around her started shuffling papers. The meeting was over. She added a few last thoughts to cover for her abstraction, and then tensed when Tino had the final word...

'I would like you all to be my guests this evening at dinner. Shall we say nine o' clock, gentlemen...and Lisa?'

He didn't look at her directly. She might have been someone he had only just met, another suit who had come to Stellamaris on the same flight as the rest. She added her own half-hearted grunt to the general murmur of acceptance, and then, collecting up her things, she started to load her briefcase.

'Lisa.'

Lisa flinched even though it was only her PA, Mike, calling to her. She was a bundle of nerves on top of everything else. That was what happened when you let your guard down—everything went to pieces. She turned around smiling, mask in place—or so she thought. Mike quickly drew her out of earshot.

'Shit, Lis'! What's happened?'

Lisa stared in amazement. Mike…beautiful Mike, with his astute blue eyes, carefully shaped brows, and expensive highlights neatly sculpted to his gorgeous, gorgeous face, never swore, never called her by a pet name, even though they had known each other for years. Was it that obvious? 'Is it obvious, Mike?' she asked him in a tense whisper, glancing around.

Taking her arm, he turned her so she faced the wall, so they both did. He put his head very close to hers, and put his arm around her protectively. 'Are you OK, Lisa? Can I do anything for you?'

What was happening to her? Lisa wondered, fighting back tears. Was she falling apart? She felt a handkerchief pressed into her hands, and nodded briskly, applying it to her mascaraed eyes as cautiously as was practicable when you were mopping up a waterfall.

'No, that's fine—you keep it,' Mike said when she absent-mindedly attempted to hand the ruined silk back to him.

She made a mental note to buy him a dozen more to replace it the moment she got back home.

'Lisa!' Mike hissed imperatively out of the corner of his mouth. 'Can I do anything for you, anything at all? Can I get you out of here?'

She saw the sense in that. 'Yes, please, Mike, that would be great.'

Putting a shielding arm out in front of her face, Mike swept them both out of the room as only he could, with *élan*, with chin tipped at a formidable angle, as if he were protecting the Queen of England from unwanted attention.

'That was a great exit,' Lisa admitted shakily when they reached the drive. Taxis were pulling up ready to take the men back to the Zagorakis guest house.

'Your voice is still wobbly,' Mike observed, 'and your face is a mess.'

'Thank you for your honesty—I think.'

'Someone has to be honest with you, Lisa.'

Lisa turned to look at him. 'You're right. I value your opinion… You do know that, don't you?'

'Thank you,' he said, preening a little. 'It's always nice to hear that you do.'

'In future, I'm going to be very different.'

'Not too different, I hope.' Mike frowned. 'There is a certain kudos in being the trusted advisor of one of the most difficult women in business today.'

'Is that what they say about me?'

'Close.'

'Hmm.' Lisa nodded thoughtfully. 'Actually, Mike, there is something else you could do for me.'

'Name it,' he said frankly.

'Sit next to me tonight. I've had enough of Zagorakis's attempts to manipulate me.'

'It would be my pleasure.'

Lisa chose the most glamorous gown she could find amongst her new clothes. It was a lacy confection that fell off one shoulder, and had a short tight skirt with a flirty tail that kicked out at one side. She brushed her hair until it gleamed like silk, and applied her make-up with unusual care—too much of it…

Far too much of it, Lisa decided, staring into the mirror. She could hear her father's sneering voice; it still haunted her. 'Your mother always wore too much make-up when she was upset.'

'And I wonder why that was, Daddy?' Lisa muttered, slapping cleansing cream onto her face.

Slipping out of the dress, she left it on the floor. Pulling on her own suit trousers and her own sensible shoes, she weakened as far as a plain ivory silk shirt was concerned when it came to plundering the collection of new clothes in her wardrobe. And that was only because she knew the evening would be warm even if they were seated outside, and she couldn't bear to be stifling in a jacket—and her own white blouse had already been taken from the room to be laundered.

She collected her hair in a loose pony-tail at the nape of her neck. Nothing too frivolous; nothing that could be construed as an attempt to win anyone's attention. Face tonic to freshen up, and then some tinted moisturiser, and a slick of lip-gloss. She confined herself to a smidgen of mascara, and a spritz of perfume later she was ready—just at the moment Mike knocked on the door.

He looked fantastic, as always. Lisa felt dowdy by comparison—and clearly looked it too, from Mike's disappointed expression.

'Oh, no… No, no, no,' he exclaimed, shaking his head. 'The minute we get back home, I'm taking you in hand.'

'I look that bad?'

'You look like a sleek, beautiful leopard masquerading as a mouse.'

'As good as that?'

'Shall we?' Mike said, offering her his arm.

Tino glanced at her, and then looked away as she walked arm in arm with Mike onto the patio. The other men were already sipping drinks, and hadn't noticed her at all. Waiters were moving amongst the small gathering with canapés, and more drinks, and absolutely everyone was in dinner suits, including Tino.

'You know what?' Mike whispered in her ear.

'What?'

'You look as out of place now as you did when you walked into the boardroom earlier today. Why don't we about-turn, and I'll sort you out?'

'Are you serious?' He clearly was, Lisa realised, when Mike wheeled her away.

As she opened the door of the first wardrobe Mike threw up his hands in a paroxysm of delight.

'Designer heaven!' He flicked expertly along the rail. 'We'll take this, and this... Oh, and this.' Holding the gossamer-fine beaded and sequinned shawl up close against his Ozwald Boateng jacket, he sighed theatrically.

Closing her eyes briefly, Lisa shook her head and smiled. She wasn't going to get out of the room again until Mike had his way—she might as well give in.

'Mike, you're my fairy godmother,' Lisa exclaimed a little while later, staring transfixed at her reflection in the full-length mirror.

'Fairy godsister, please... Well, what do you think?'

'What do you think is more to the point,' Lisa said, turning around to smile at him.

'Well, that brute of a Greek isn't going to ignore you now, that's for sure,' he said with satisfaction, offering Lisa his arm.

Mike made her pause just inside the door where the light was a little brighter than on the patio. There wasn't quite an audible gasp, but there might as well have been. Every man had turned to stare.

Mike had dressed her hair high so that she looked taller than usual, and a few softening tendrils had been allowed to escape around her carefully made-up face. Mike had designed her make-up too, to complete the 'look', as he called it, with all the care he might have applied to one of his famously fabulous room settings. Her eyes were smoky, her lashes black… Her lips were full and glossy red, and there was just a hint of rouge to define her cheekbones—the end result? She looked like something out of *Vogue* or *Tatler*—anyway, quite unlike herself, Lisa decided.

She had never gone for full-on glamour in her life before, but, of course, Mike did nothing by halves. The strappy sandals he'd insisted she wear had stratospheric heels, and the dress he had chosen was cut, appropriately enough, with a nod to ancient Grecian styling. Cunningly draped, it fitted where it touched, and was extremely elegant, yet sexy—with a slit up the side to a point where Lisa felt quite a draft, especially as Mike had specifically ruled out the wearing of underwear.

Seeing Tino swallow, she rejoiced.

'Up yours, Zagorakis,' Mike murmured, showing his own feelings were somewhat less subtle.

'Mike, please,' Lisa whispered, finding a smile had crept onto her own lips. 'Gentlemen,' she said casually, dipping her head minutely to acknowledge everyone.

There was a stampede to be the first to find her a drink, a canapé, a seat if she wanted one; only Tino stood back, his face a mask she couldn't read.

The evening was delightful, the food delicious—or that would have been the press-release version, Lisa realised cynically, glancing at Tino. Having chosen a seat as far away from her as possible, he was deep in conversation with his financial director.

'I shall sulk.'

Lisa turned as Mike spoke to her.

'I've gone to all this trouble and you're staring at him like a lovesick ninny. Honestly, Lisa, if he wasn't so gorgeous, I'd be quite put out.'

'I'm sorry, Mike.' She touched his arm. 'Was I being so obvious?'

'Well, luckily for you, he didn't notice. He's far too busy talking business.'

'Time to mingle again,' she suggested.

The dinner was over, last dregs of coffee and brandy had been drunk. Mike half rose—Lisa stopped him, putting her hand on his arm. 'Mike, can I come back with you to the guest house?'

'Of course…but why?'

'Well, I've been staying here at the villa.'

'I know.'

'And now…'

Mike held his hands up to silence her. 'You don't have to say another word—as long as you're quite sure about this?'

Lisa followed Mike's gaze to where she could see Tino turning on the charm. He looked fiendishly fabulous: stronger, taller, and more interesting than any other man present, talking easily to everyone, except her. She caught a flash of white teeth as he responded to another man's comment, and then a fierce, black-eyed stare when he caught her looking at him. 'I'm absolutely sure.'

'OK, then, but we have to brave the receiving line, or whatever the opposite of that might be,' Mike informed her briskly. 'Come along, darling, everyone else is starting to leave now. You just stay with me, and I'll see you through it safely.'

There were some things even Mike couldn't fix.

'Where do you think you're going?' Tino said.

'I'm going to the guest house with Mike.'

Instead of arguing with her, Tino took hold of Mike's elbow, and drew him to one side, leaving Lisa standing alone out of earshot. And when Mike half turned to her, Tino put his hand on his arm and drew him back again to say something more. To Lisa's amazement, Mike, her right-hand man, her PA, her friend, walked away without another word, and when she tried to go after him Tino caught hold of her arm and held her back.

'What the hell do you think you're doing?' she demanded, looking down at his hand on her arm.

'I might ask you the same question,' he replied icily.

'It's clear you don't want me here, so I'm going to where I am wanted.'

'You're talking like a spoiled brat, Lisa.'

He led her back inside the house, and closed the door. 'Did you have to make such an exhibition of yourself?'

'Do you have to hold my arm so tightly?'

He released her immediately. 'You'd better come into my study and we'll talk there.'

'We've nothing to discuss.'

'So, this is the thanks I get?'

'Thanks? For what?' Lisa demanded incredulously. 'For making a fool out of me?' She tried to push past him and go outside again to find Mike, but he blocked the door.

'All this is for you, Lisa.'

'And you didn't think to tell me you had called my people over?'

'I wanted to surprise you.'

'Well, you certainly did that.'

'I tried to find you…I tried to warn you they were here, but no one knew where you were.'

Lisa smiled bitterly. 'Maybe because I was doing something for you.'

'What?'

'It really doesn't matter now.' She reached past him to the door handle. 'Let me out of here now, Tino.'

'Or what?'

'I call for the police, and tell them you're holding me against my will?'

Tino held her stare. 'On Stellamaris, I *am* the police.'

'Well, I'm happy for you. Now will you call for a taxi to take me to the guest house, or do I have to make that call?'

Seizing her arm, he marched her down the corridor towards his study. When they got inside, he slammed the door and stood with his back to it. 'Would you mind telling me what all this is about?' His angry gesture encompassed every inch of Lisa, from her beautifully coiffed hair to her shell-pink toenails peeping out of the glamorous sandals, and before she could answer he added, 'Did you have to make such a show of yourself in front of all those men?'

'Are you jealous, Tino?'

'Jealous? Of a tramp?'

Her stinging blow caught him full on the face, shooting his head back. He stared at her in total disbelief, nursing his chin.

Lisa could hardly believe what she had done. She hated violence of any sort. She despised it. And now she had sunk to the lowest level possible. It didn't matter that Tino thoroughly deserved it; nothing would ever excuse such a loss of control. 'I should never have done that.'

'You pack quite a punch.' He nursed his chin.

'That was unforgivable.' She had never lost control before, not even to the extent where she had cursed at someone. She didn't know herself any more, and she didn't like the person she had become.

'I'm sorry too.'

She looked at him.

'I shouldn't have called you those names.'

They were apologising to each other? What was happening? They had plumbed the extremes of emotion together, and now the carefully controlled Tino Zagorakis was bending towards the equally unyielding Lisa Bond?

'Stay on.'

'What?' Now she *was* astonished.

'Stay on at the Villa Aphrodite until Friday, as we agreed. We haven't finished our discussions yet—and this is a big place, Lisa. I'll keep out of your way; you keep out of mine.'

If there had only been business between them, that would have made perfect sense... And there was only business between them, Lisa reminded herself. Tino had just made that clear. So, why couldn't she stay?

But where had it all gone? Where had all the passion and tenderness gone? If this was the life expectancy of the average love affair, she could do without them. She should have known the closeness between them was only an illusion. As Jack Bond had said when he'd thrown earth on her mother's coffin: 'Any woman who expects too much out of life is destined to be disappointed.'

CHAPTER NINE

WHEN she woke the next morning Lisa lay in bed propped up on pillows, staring at the sea, knowing she would never be able to look at the ocean again without thinking about the day she spent on Tino's boat...

For that one short day they had been so close... Thinking that would last was as foolish as expecting the morning mist to hang around. They were both far too sensible to get close to anyone. She had just been swept away by the madness that affected many women from cold northern climes—she had seen another way of life, another type of man, and imagined that she could slip easily into his world.

Hearing a tap on the door, she slid out of bed. Grabbing a robe, she hurried to find the same friendly young maid standing outside.

'Would you like to take breakfast on your balcony again this morning, Thespinis Bond?'

Lisa hesitated. Why should she be confined to barracks? She had reached an accommodation with Tino. There was no reason why she shouldn't go down for breakfast. There were still a few points she wanted to discuss with him off the record before their teams joined them later. 'Would it be any trouble to you if I had my breakfast downstairs, Maria?'

'No trouble at all, Thespinis Bond. I will set a place for you on the patio right away.'

Another new outfit! It couldn't be helped, Lisa thought as she checked her appearance in the mirror. She would pay back Tino for everything she had worn, and then perhaps negotiate directly with the boutiques for the other clothes and accessories. Everything was so beautiful, it was hard to let any of it go.

Lisa's heart was thumping as she walked onto the patio. It didn't matter what type of agreement she had agreed to; after all that had happened between them she still had a lot of readjusting to do.

'*Kalimera*, Lisa.'

There was no sign of Tino. Lisa didn't know whether to be relieved or not, but she was happy to see Stella Panayotakis sitting at the breakfast table… 'I didn't expect to see you today, Stella. What a lovely surprise.'

'For me too,' Stella assured her. 'Won't you join me?'

She indicated the place next to her, and Lisa saw that this was the only other place set at the table.

'Tino will not be joining us this morning,' Stella explained, seeing her glance. 'He's been called away.'

'I see…' Called away? Avoiding her after everything that had happened between them was more likely, she suspected.

'Tino didn't tell you?'

'No, and we're supposed to be holding meetings all this week.' She couldn't keep the tension out of her voice.

'I am sure Constantine would not have left the island unless it was important, Lisa.'

'I'm sure you're right, Stella. But I can't understand why he just didn't warn me. I'm sorry, Stella, I know this isn't your fault, but the issues I have come here to discuss with him are really important. And Tino is just so…unpredictable. Nothing happens without his approval.'

'Please don't get upset—and you don't need to apologise. I can see how much this means to you.' Sitting back in her chair, Stella stared at Lisa in silence for a moment. 'The people in your company are very lucky to have you for their champion, Lisa.'

Stella's endorsement only made Lisa more aware of the

responsibility she had towards her co-workers at Bond Steel. 'Do you know how I can get in touch with him? Do you know where Tino's gone, Stella?'

'I'm afraid I can't help you, Lisa.'

Can't help me, or won't help me? Lisa wondered, sensing Stella was watching her words as if she was protecting Tino for some reason.

'What time is your first meeting this morning?'

Stella's question prompted Lisa to refocus on the older woman's face. 'Ten o'clock.'

'But it's only eight o'clock. Why don't you come down to the beach with me for a stroll before you start work? You never know, Lisa—Constantine may have been in contact with his household by the time you return to the villa.'

'I'd love to come with you.' Lisa sighed.

'Then why not indulge yourself for once?'

'All right.' She smiled. It was hard not to when Stella was around.

'Shouldn't you change first?' Stella suggested, glancing at Lisa's elegant outfit.

'Will you give me five minutes?'

'Of course.'

They took the funicular down to the beach. 'It's great to be able to admire the view without picking your way down the cliff face,' Lisa admitted wryly.

'You should never do that, Lisa!' Stella warned. 'That cliff is for mountain goats, and crazy men like Tino.'

Lisa seized the opening: 'Have you known Tino for long?'

'It seems like for ever.' Stella quickly became guarded again. 'Look,' she said, pointing out to sea. 'Can you see the dolphins, Lisa?'

Stella's adroit change of subject didn't bode well for discovering facts about Tino. Her reluctance to talk about him made Lisa more certain than ever that both of them were hiding something.

When they reached the beach and the doors slid open, the first thing Lisa saw was another couple. Engrossed in each other, they were standing at the water's edge with their fingers entwined. The young woman's face turned up to her dark-haired companion was like a pale flame in the morning light. A stab of jealousy made Lisa hesitate and want to turn back. Had Tino been lying to her all along? And Stella too? No, not Stella…Stella would *never* lie to her. But she didn't want to see… She didn't want to be sure… She couldn't bear to be so cruelly disillusioned. 'I'm sorry, Stella. I should never have come down to the beach. There really isn't time… I should go back and prepare for the meeting.'

'You work too hard, Lisa. You should make a little time for yourself.'

Lisa's glance slipped back to the couple standing at the water's edge.

Misreading her interest, Stella grabbed hold of her arm, and started to lead her across the sands. 'You must meet my daughter.'

'Arianna and I have already met—briefly, at the villa when I first arrived.'

'Then let me introduce you properly,' Stella insisted, giving Lisa's arm a little tug.

It wasn't Tino! *It wasn't Tino…* As they drew closer and Lisa saw her mistake she instantly regretted her suspicions, and when Stella began the introductions she discovered that, like Arianna, Giorgio was also an opera singer, an Italian tenor of some renown. He and Arianna were due to start a week's rehearsals for a major new production at the Covent Garden Opera House in London. Of course, that was why Stella had been staying at the villa, Lisa realised.

She had wanted to give the two lovers some space, before world attention intruded on their personal lives.

'I have something to ask you, Stella.'

Lisa looked up at Arianna's handsome companion, and then looked at Stella.

'Not yet, Giorgio,' Stella warned, her eyes twinkling.

'No,' Arianna agreed. 'We must wait for Tino.'

Wait for Tino? Lisa's mouth hardened. Why did he have to be part of this? Could no deal be struck, not even a love match, without his seal of approval? Why should Arianna's happiness depend on him? She couldn't understand it. Surely Stella's approval was all that mattered?

'Arianna is right, Giorgio,' Stella said, 'You must be patient. We have to wait for Tino to return.'

With a heartfelt groan, Giorgio looked for some relief from Arianna, but she only shrugged and kissed him impulsively on the cheek. 'Waiting will make everything that much better,' she insisted.

Every mention of Tino's name was like a burr in Lisa's side. It was growing increasingly hard to hide her feelings. 'How long do you expect Tino to be away from the island, Stella?'

'He will be back when he has finished his other business.'

Arianna's face lit up with understanding. 'Ah, so Tino has gone to the—'

'Arianna!' Stella silenced her daughter with a look. 'We will talk about this later.'

Why had they all turned to stare at her now? Lisa wondered. Why was she being left out of the loop? Didn't any of them trust her? She held in her feelings, but it seemed as good a time as any to leave. 'It's been lovely meeting you, Giorgio, and seeing you again, Stella, Arianna—' she glanced apologetically at her shorts and bare feet '—but I really have to go now.'

'I guess that's not your business uniform?' Giorgio suggested.

'Next time you must share our breakfast,' Arianna offered warmly.

She had been wrong to doubt any of them, Lisa realised, but where Tino was concerned she couldn't think straight. 'I'd love to.' But there wouldn't be another time, Lisa realised, giving Stella an impulsive hug. Breaking away, she ran across the beach without glancing back.

As the funicular took her slowly up the cliff Lisa noticed the three figures were still standing in the same place waving to her, but then her vision blurred and she couldn't see them any longer.

As Lisa had suspected, the meeting soon reached a point where Tino's presence was essential. No one breathed at Zagorakis Inc without his say-so—and time was running out. 'I think we'll have to call it a day here, gentlemen.'

'My apologies everyone. I hope the meeting went OK without me?'

Lisa stared. Tino had just walked into the room as if he had never been away. 'Yes, what a shame you missed it.' She reached for her briefcase. Five days…*five lousy days*, were all they had agreed upon—and he couldn't even make it past two.

'That will be all, everyone. We will reconvene tomorrow.'

Lisa tensed as he took control, adding her own rider, 'Yes, thank you everyone.'

As the men filed out Tino pointed to the chair she had just vacated.

'The meeting is over, Tino.'

'And I want to hear what went on.'

'I'm sure one of your team will fill you in.' Picking up her briefcase, she tried to move past him.

'But I want you to tell me.'

'OK, then, shut the door.' She stayed where she was while he crossed the room to see to it. 'You couldn't even be bothered to make the meeting, so why are you so interested now in what went on?'

'My interest in the deal has never wavered.'

'Unlike your interest in our agreement?'

Leaning back on the door, he stared at her. 'Stop this, Lisa. I called the meeting, didn't I?'

'So you should have been here when it started—except you couldn't be, because you had to be somewhere else, somewhere more important.'

'I thought it was agreed that we have no hold over each other.'

'No hold over each other? So, that night we spent in bed was simply recreation for you—a little pleasure on the side? Didn't you think there might be consequences?'

'Consequences? Why should there be consequences? I took precautions.'

Lisa's face flamed red. Tino was always top of the class where practicalities were concerned. He had wanted a few guilt-free hours of pleasure, of release—it meant no more to him than that. But was she any better? She had lost control, and now she had to pay the price—but not for very much longer. 'You'll have to find someone else to fill you in on the meeting, Tino.'

He stood aside to let her pass, but as she swept past he reached out and stopped her. 'Are you coming to the dinner tonight?'

'At the fish restaurant? No—I'm going to start my packing this evening.' She stared coldly at his hand on her arm.

'Of course, you must have a lot of things to pack. Would you like me to have some extra suitcases brought to your room?'

She reddened, second-guessing his thoughts. 'I'm going

to pay you for everything. It's all—' She stopped, feeling awkward.

'Chosen with care,' he murmured sardonically.

She knew that wasn't true. Holding his gaze, she smiled faintly. They really were as bad as each other. 'I can just imagine.'

'So, we'll meet again tomorrow morning?'

This time Tino not only stood back, but held the door wide for her, and Lisa felt that deserved a little information: 'We may be able to sign before Friday—things went really well this morning.'

'I shall have to confirm that with my team.'

Wasn't her word good enough? She firmed her voice. 'And I'll be leaving the moment we sign.'

'We have an agreement.'

'An agreement you broke.'

'I'm here now.'

'That's hardly the point. You were the one who said we couldn't cherry-pick agreements.'

'I had to be somewhere else.' His mouth flattened uncompromisingly.

Secrets…always secrets. 'You can't just bend our agreement to suit yourself.'

'I'd say we've got a pretty good agreement. Didn't you say we're about to cut a deal in record time?'

'I'll see you tomorrow, Tino.'

He stood in her way.

'Do you mind?' She waited, but this time he didn't stand aside.

Closing the door, he locked it. 'What the hell do you think you're doing?'

'I have another proposition for you.'

'It's too late for that, Tino. I've got everything I could possibly want from you.'

'I don't think so,' he argued softly.

'I must have missed something.'

'What have you missed, Lisa? This?'

Before she could respond he dragged her close. She whipped her face away when he tried to kiss her.

'Let's get rid of this first.' Seizing her briefcase, he tossed it onto a chair.

'What do you think you're doing? Don't play games with me, Tino! Let me out of here right now.'

'If I thought you really wanted to leave, I'd let you go immediately.'

'You don't know what I want.' She fought him. 'I don't believe this.'

'Do you believe this?'

Holding her firm with one hand, he cupped her face with the other and brushed her mouth with his lips until he drew a ragged moan from the very depths of her soul. 'I don't think you want to leave just yet, do you, Lisa?'

She was trembling as he teased the seam of her mouth with his tongue, and then because she wanted to, because she had to, because she couldn't stop herself, she pressed herself against him, and then her mind was wiped clean of everything but the need to have sex with him.

Tino removed her tailored trousers in one easy movement with the cobweb-fine briefs she was wearing under them. She gasped with relief hearing the foil package rip. 'Oh, yes, please.' And burrowed her face into his chest as he lifted her…

It was the most reckless thing she had ever done. The windows were unshuttered, the drapes fully open. Anyone walking past couldn't miss what was happening inside the room. It only fuelled her excitement.

Tino lowered her down on top of the boardroom table and lifted her legs to lock them around his waist.

'This is madness.'

'Yes, isn't it?' he agreed.

He was so matter-of-fact he made her mad for him, and when his warm breath tickled her ear she shuddered uncontrollably.

'This is what you want, isn't it, Lisa? It's what we both want.'

Her eyes were growing heavy-lidded with desire. 'It's what we both need,' she agreed throatily.

'Oh, yes, we need it,' Tino murmured as he passed the tip of his erection between her legs. 'You're so wet.'

She leaned back against his arm at a better angle for him.

'You're so beautiful,' he teased, drawing back a little, 'maybe I'll just look at you instead.'

'Don't, Tino,' Lisa warned. 'I can't wait any longer.'

'In that case…'

A low moan of pleasure flowed from her lips as he eased himself into her.

'Better?'

'Much, much better,' Lisa agreed, closing her muscles around him as her voice tailed away. She felt wonderful…he completed her…

'There's no hurry…just relax, and enjoy yourself.'

He behaved as if they had all day, as if they were alone on the island! 'But if anyone should come around the back of the villa—'

'The only person who is going to come is you, and, after that, me.'

His tone was dry and amused, but Lisa detected a strand of tension. The possibility of discovery excited him, she realised. 'You have less to lose than I do if we are discovered.'

'Is that so?' He thrust deep, forcing her to collapse against him with a groan of delight.

'It's true,' she managed to gasp. 'You will be hailed as a stud, whereas I—'

'Talk far too much.'

If Tino hadn't been holding her so securely she might have slipped to the floor, Lisa realised as they both recovered from what had been a shattering climax. She was reluctant to let him go, reluctant to stand alone, reluctant to lose the warmth of his body, and the wonderful feeling of security his strength always gave her.

'Do you feel a little better now?' he teased softly, nuzzling his rough chin against her neck.

'A little better.'

'But not fully sated?'

'Are you?' She let her hands slide up his arms, relishing the feel of naked power flexing beneath her searching fingertips.

Tino smiled as he eased out of her, and then he looked past her out of the window. 'What perfect timing.' Moving in front of Lisa, he shielded her.

Then she saw the group of men heading for the beach. 'You knew,' she breathed incredulously. 'You knew they could walk past here at any moment.'

'Don't tell me the possibility of discovery didn't excite you too?'

She couldn't admit that it had.

'Do you think I got all this by being cautious?' he gestured around.

'No, I don't suppose you did.' But did she want to become part of his risk culture?

'So, Lisa—do you still want to rush back to the UK when we sign the contract?'

Truthfully, no. Even with all the warnings she'd been giving herself she still wanted him. She wanted him so badly she knew it was dangerous…out of control. 'I must reassure everyone at Bond Steel as soon as I can.' That was the perfect excuse—so why couldn't she just turn away from him and stay safe?

'You can let them know any number of ways,' Tino pointed out. 'Or you could just send Mike home with the good news. I'm sure he'd like that.'

'I'm sure he would. But why should I stay here with you?'

'Because you want to.'

She held his gaze, wondering if it was safe for her heart to beat so fast. 'You're very sure of yourself.'

'Forty-eight hours of sexual excess? Sounds tempting to me.'

As her gaze strayed to Tino's mouth Lisa knew he was right.

'It's perfect for us, Lisa—no strings, no consequences… I can't offer you the long term, and I know that's the last thing you're looking for.'

In that moment something died inside her, but something far more elemental took its place. 'I'm not sure if I should stay.'

'Yes, you are,' he said confidently. 'And just think of it—we'll be all alone when the others leave the island.'

'Except for your staff.'

'Who are well schooled in discretion. We will be able to extend our area of study into all the extremes of erotic adventure.' He smiled against her mouth. 'We're the same, you and I, Lisa; don't fight it. Looking at you is like looking in the mirror. I don't always like what I see, but at least I always know what you're thinking.'

She wanted sex with him so desperately it was like a kind of madness, but even more than that she longed to be close to him…even though she knew Tino was never going to let that happen.

'So? Give me your answer, Lisa. Do you accept my proposition?'

Gazing up at him, she saw that his warm, wonderful eyes had turned black with erotic promise.

'I accept.'

CHAPTER TEN

THRUSTING his face into his hands, Tino made a rough, animal sound as he paced his room. What was he turning into? What the hell was Lisa turning him into? Right now, he was no better than a rutting beast scenting a female ripe for sex.

And now he was blaming Lisa for his own weakness! As he stood in the centre of his study his face contorted with anger and disgust. What kind of a man did that make him? Was it Lisa's fault that he only had to look at her, or think about her, and he turned into that most primal of men—a man who could think of nothing but possession, and sex?

He couldn't think about business, or Stellamaris, or about any of his other responsibilities, because she filled his every waking moment, as well as his dreams at night. He could see no further than keeping her with him every precious second he could until they both returned to their cold, emotion-free lives. While she was in Stellamaris he could fill his eyes with every nuance and quirk in her expression, fill his nostrils with her scent, and his hands with her silky flesh... He couldn't let her go, not yet. That accounted for his preposterous scheme—an erotic adventure for the next forty-eight hours? He couldn't believe he had suggested it. And he only had because he wasn't capable of committing to anything more, and that shamed him.

They'd shared explosive sex, which accounted for an erotic adventure being the first thing that sprang into his mind, but they'd shared some tender moments too. As he remembered those now his mouth flattened with despair.

He would have done better to take her on a tour of the island. He of all people knew how dangerous it was to play with anyone's feelings—and he had no excuse; he knew she was as scarred as he was. And what? Did he want to hurt her more? The best thing he could have done for Lisa was to stay away from her for good.

In just one day more their business dealings would be concluded. Of course the deal was done. For the first time in his business career he hadn't listened to his advisors, to his own intuition, or to the bald facts as they appeared in columns of figures on the documents that lay untouched on his desk. He could see no further than the fact that Lisa's company desperately needed a cash injection from him, and that he wouldn't let her fail.

She could have had anything she wanted from him, but he knew she would only take what she needed to secure the future of her people. He had been wrong to say they were alike when he was still holding himself aloof, still keeping his true feelings hidden.

He smiled grimly, remembering all the clothes he had ordered for her. He hadn't troubled to choose them himself. Of course he hadn't. When had he ever taken time to do that—even for himself? Money bought more than fabulous clothes, and fast cars, it bought the undivided attention of top people in whatever field he chose to spread his wealth.

Delegating trivia like shopping had always worked fine for him before. He didn't care as long as there was always a clean shirt waiting, but now it wasn't enough. He wanted to choose something special for Lisa, and he wanted to do that without anyone else's interference. He wanted her to have something precious, something unique, something to remember him by.

Making a harsh noise that sounded nothing like a laugh, Tino stared at himself in the mirror, his mouth twisting with self-disgust.

'Come in, Maria.' Lisa recognised the knock on her bedroom door. She was almost ready for dinner, and it was always a pleasure to see the young girl.

'Why, Maria, you look beautiful.'

'We can never wait for anything here in Stellamaris, so the celebrations for May Day have already started in our village,' Maria explained, spreading her hands lovingly down her intricately embroidered skirt. 'We are all in national costume.'

'Well, I think you look absolutely stunning. What a wonderful heritage.'

'You look very lovely too, Thespinis Bond,' Maria said, her black eyes widening as Lisa stood up.

'Thank you, Maria. I only hope Kirie Zagorakis will think so. He bought this dress for me.' Lisa blushed, realising that she had confessed rather more than she ought to, but the jade-green chiffon, though more modest than some of the other gowns in her wardrobe, was perhaps the most beautiful dress she had ever owned, and tonight, in spite of their pact, she wanted Tino to look at her with something other than lust in his eyes.

'What's that, Maria?' Apprehension struck Lisa as she stared at the velvet box in Maria's hands.

'Kirie Zagorakis asked me to bring this to you, Thespinis Bond. He asks you to put them on for him this evening.'

Lisa frowned as she stared at the small velvet case Maria was holding out to her. Maria frowned too, sensing her unease.

'Just leave it over there.' Lisa pointed to her dressing table. She couldn't bring herself to open the small case in front of anyone, not even Maria.

As Maria did as she asked Lisa stepped forward impulsively, and took the young girl's hands between her own. 'You've been very kind to me, Maria.'

'Kind to you?' Maria looked at her with surprise, tilting

up her chin to stare into Lisa's eyes, 'Is no one else kind to you, Thespinis Bond?'

'Of course, they are, Maria.' Lisa looked away briefly. 'But you've made me feel so welcome here.'

Turning at the door, Maria smiled at her. 'I hope you have a lovely evening, Thespinis Bond.'

Lisa circled the jewellery box as if it were an asp. It was just a small box in navy-blue velvet, she told herself sensibly... A small, beautifully made box that looked as if it had come from one of the most exclusive jewellers in Athens. But how could that be possible? Had it been delivered by jet, or by helicopter? Or did Tino keep a stock of such things, just in case—perhaps increasing the value of the gift depending upon the services he had received? The blood drained from her face at the thought of the pleasure they had shared. Was this her payment for it?

Lisa looked at the jewel case again. She wanted to believe it was a spontaneous gift with no strings attached; something she could return without causing offence. She had last seen Tino five hours ago. Plenty of time for a wilful billionaire to call for his jet to go shopping...

But that wasn't Tino's way, Lisa remembered. He ordered in: designer clothes, accessories, jewels, like other men ordered pizza. The amethyst earrings had been a perfect example. Was he upping the ante now, perhaps tempting her with priceless baubles to see if he could push her into becoming the billionaire's bought woman? Exhaling tensely, she picked up the box, and checked her pale reflection one last time in the mirror.

The return of the gift, as well as the confrontation she expected to erupt between them—none of that was possible, Lisa realised as soon as she walked onto the patio. Tonight was clearly a night of celebration for Arianna and Giorgio.

She didn't need anyone to tell her that Tino had given

his permission for the two of them to marry; the joy on each of their faces told its own story.

'Lisa,' Arianna said happily, hurrying forward to draw her into the tightly knit group. 'Giorgio and I are to be married.'

'I'm so happy for you,' Lisa said sincerely. Drawing Arianna to her, she held her close for a moment. She knew Tino was standing just a few feet away. 'Giorgio,' she said, releasing Arianna, 'you're a very lucky man.'

'I know that, Lisa,' Giorgio assured her as he put a protective arm around Arianna's waist.

Tearing her gaze away from them, Lisa went next to Stella, and took both the older woman's outstretched hands in her own, 'This must be a very happy day for you.'

'This is the happiest day of my life,' Stella admitted, dragging Lisa into a bear hug. 'And now I only have one task left to complete on Cupid's behalf.'

'Which is?'

The sound of Tino's voice made Lisa tense in Stella's arms.

'Why,' Stella said, turning from Lisa to Tino, 'I would have thought that was obvious, Constantine. I still have to find someone who will marry you.'

'That is one task far better left undone,' he said softly.

Stella's noncommittal hum made them all laugh.

'Shall we sit down?' Stella suggested. Pointing to a chair, she indicated that Lisa should sit next to Tino.

Discreetly, Lisa put the small velvet case on the table between them.

'Do you want me to put them on for you?' He leaned across.

'No. I do not want you to put them on for me,' Lisa said under her breath, 'whatever *they* might be.'

'You mean you haven't looked?' His voice rose. 'You mean you haven't even opened my gift.'

Everyone was staring at them.

'Forgive me, Stella Panayotakis, Arianna, Giorgio,' he said smoothly. 'I did not mean to interrupt your conversation.'

'Is that a gift for Lisa?' Stella said happily. 'You should give it to her yourself, Tino.'

'No, no, I—'Lisa started to protest as she pushed her chair back from the table. But then she felt Tino's hand on her arm and froze. She couldn't do this. Of course she couldn't do this. She couldn't ruin Arianna's evening. 'Forgive me, everyone.' She found a laugh. 'I've never been very good at receiving gifts.'

'Perhaps that's because you haven't received enough gifts,' Stella remarked, busying herself with some olive-oil dip for her bread.

'What have you bought for Lisa, Tino?' Arianna cut in, dispelling the tension with her excitement. 'I love presents. And, Giorgio—I'm very good at receiving them.'

Everyone laughed, and then Arianna said, 'Well, aren't you going to show us what you have bought for Lisa, Tino?'

He shrugged, and flipped the catch on the jewel case.

There was a stunned silence. The perfectly matched emerald earrings were surrounded by brilliant cut diamonds.

Giorgio was the first to recover. 'Why, they're magnificent,' he said bluntly. 'I've never seen such splendid stones.'

They were everything she had been expecting, and dreading too, Lisa realised as she watched Tino pluck the earrings from their velvet nest.

'I remembered how much you loved the amethysts,' he murmured, brushing back her hair to fix one earring in place. 'And I thought these would be even better, because they will bring out the colour of your eyes.' Cupping her chin in one hand, he brought her round to face him so that Lisa had nowhere to look but straight into his.

'There…I was right,' he murmured, adjusting the second one. 'They're perfect.'

There was a spontaneous round of applause.

She knew he could see the tears building up in her eyes, and she hated herself for the weakness. It took every ounce of will-power and years of practice to hold them back. 'Thank you.' Her voice sounded so wooden. 'The earrings are lovely.'

'And now we go dancing in the village to celebrate,' Stella declared energetically.

'Will you excuse me?' Lisa pushed up from the table. 'I seem to have developed a slight headache… The flickering candles, perhaps.'

'Lisa—' Tino started to get up from the table too, and then Arianna did too.

Stella held her daughter back. 'You must be exhausted, Lisa. I know what these meetings have meant to you. Business has taken everything out of you. You need rest now…rest, and quiet..and, goodness knows, you won't get that in the village. Tino,' Stella said, turning to him, 'see that you take care of Lisa. She must go to bed with a cup of warm milk.'

'Of course, Stella,' he murmured politely, giving her a small bow.

Was this payback time for the priceless emeralds? Lisa wondered, because, however much she wanted Tino, she could never be bought.

They both stood as still as statues until Stella, Arianna and Giorgio had gone, and then Tino turned to her. 'I'm not sure about the cup of warm milk.'

'Tino, don't.'

'What do you mean, don't?' he said, lifting his warm hands away from her shoulders.

Taking off the earrings, Lisa held them out to him. 'I don't need these.'

'No one *needs* beautiful things, but they are an expression of…'

'Of what, Tino?' Lisa said tensely. 'Possession?'

She could see he was shocked. Perhaps she had gone straight to the heart of the matter. 'Please take them back, Tino. I can't take them. If I did want some new jewellery, I would buy it for myself.'

'But it gave me such pleasure to buy them for you.'

Lisa almost smiled, but it would have been a sad smile. Tino sounded like a small child who couldn't have his own way. They were both spoiled. They spoiled themselves. They had both reached a point where they could buy anything they wanted. And none of it mattered, none of it counted for anything. They were always flailing around thinking that the next purchase would fill the gap in their hearts, but it never did. 'You bought the earrings for me? Did you pick them out yourself? Or did you make a telephone call, and have someone else do that?'

'I took the jet.' His mouth curved a little in wry appreciation of the privileged position in which he found himself.

'So, you did choose them.'

'Yes, of course I did—there's no need to sound so surprised.' Opening his fist, Tino stared down at the priceless gems nestled there. 'I thought you'd like them.'

'I do like them, but—' How could she put her thoughts into words? They were both hopeless, both so clumsy when it came to managing the simplest of human relationships—and theirs was scarcely that. They matched perfectly sexually but something inside was broken—for both of them. 'If you had wanted to give me a gift, why didn't you give me some flowers from the garden, Tino? Like you did before…that would have been lovely.'

'But I wanted to buy you something really special.'

'The flowers were special…but emerald earrings?' Lisa searched for the right words, words that would make sense to a billionaire to whom priceless emeralds would make no more dent in his bank account than another yacht. 'I feel as if you're trying to buy me, Tino—as if you're trying to pay me for my services.' She made a gesture of frustration.

'Your services?' Now he did smile. 'Please.' He held the earrings out to her again. 'Take them back as payment on account.'

'This isn't a joke, Tino.'

'I agree with you.' He lowered his voice. 'Take them, Lisa, I beg you.'

'You beg?' She shook her head. 'Put them away before you lose them, Tino. They will have to be returned. I'm sorry, but you have flown to Athens for nothing.'

'For nothing?' His mouth tugged up wickedly at one corner. 'Are you sure?'

'The earrings must be returned to the jeweller, Tino. We've both made mistakes. We're both useless when it comes to knowing what to do, how to behave in situations that don't involve business.'

'Is that what we have between us—a situation?'

'Today is Wednesday and I'm going home on Friday. Let's not make any more of this than we should…please, no more grand gestures, Tino.'

'No more flying to Athens to buy you jewellery, you mean?'

As he gazed at her she saw a glint of humour had returned to his eyes. She pulled away. 'You must be exhausted, after your journey.'

'Not too tired to want you in my bed.' He dragged her back into his arms. 'And I will have my own way on this—with or without emerald earrings, you and I have an agreement to fulfil.'

He carried her upstairs, and, shouldering open the door to his suite, took her straight to the bed.

Lisa watched as he tugged off his shirt. 'Tino, please, this doesn't feel right.'

'Why should we waste time when time is running out? We should make the most of it, don't you think?'

'I just can't do this.' Lisa tensed, expecting him to react to having his male pride badly dented, but instead he surprised her, coming to kneel at the side of the bed.

Taking her hand in his, he raised it to his forehead and closed his eyes. 'Lisa, I'm so sorry… You're right—we're both hopeless cases. Can you forgive me?' He looked up.

'You'll take the earrings back to the jeweller's?'

'If you really don't want them,' he agreed, searching her face. 'I'll do anything for you.'

Yes, but only for the duration of their agreement, Lisa thought sadly. And then Tino smiled at her, and the delicious curve of his mouth, and the laughter in his eyes, won her over.

She would have been frightened of a man like this at one time, Lisa realised, a man who could make her do anything he wanted with his strength alone, but it was the need she saw in him, the need that so perfectly matched her own that made her weaken…

He saw the change in her at once, and eased up from his knees. 'You can't resist me?' he proposed wickedly.

'Was there ever a more arrogant man on the face of this earth?'

'Not here, surely?' He looked at her wryly, and then gazed around. 'I'm standing in the middle of my own bedroom.'

'Then come to me,' Lisa suggested seductively.

Was lovemaking supposed to start with shrieks of laughter, and end like this? Lisa wondered, lying snug in Tino's arms. He had just dropped off to sleep, as well he might after the exertions of the day—and she didn't just have flying in mind, she reflected mischievously, brushing a stray lock of inky-black hair from his eyes. He moaned softly with contentment, and shifted position slightly at her side, drawing her a little closer.

'I think I love you, Tino Zagorakis.' She was safe in the knowledge that he couldn't hear her—but she did love him, Lisa realised with a jolt of happiness. He was everything to her. Tino was everything she had ever dreamed of and far more than she could ever have imagined. He made her laugh…he made sex fun and safe—and he'd found a use for the emerald earrings, though not the use the high-class jeweller would have had in mind when he'd secured the sale… If the jeweller discovered where those earrings had been clipped Tino would never be able to return them!

Burrowing her face into Tino's chest, Lisa kissed him tenderly, but she had disturbed him, and he stirred restlessly, pushing her away in his sleep.

'No…I don't want to.' He thrashed his head on the pillow.

'What don't you want to do, my love?' she said softly, tracing the line of his mouth very gently with her fingertip.

'Don't hurt me.' The words jerked out of him, muddled and indistinct.

Resting up on one elbow, Lisa stared down feeling increasingly alarmed. 'Tino? Are you asleep?' He was fast asleep, she realised, and he was held fast in the grip of some awful dream. 'Tino, please, wake up.'

Lisa's heart was thundering in her chest as Tino shook her off.

'No!' he exclaimed louder than before, jerking away from her.

'Tino!' Shaking his arm, she raised her voice, hoping to get through to him.

'Leave me... Go away... Get out of here!'

His voice, still muffled by the pillows, was barely deci-
pherable. But she knew now that he wasn't speaking to her,
he was still locked in the dream—and there was something
horribly reminiscent of the commune about it.

But surely Tino hadn't lived in a commune? That was
too much of a coincidence to swallow, and the world would
have heard of it by now—as her past had been played out
in the glossies and tabloids. So, what, then? From the little
Lisa could unravel, she gathered someone was trying to
force him to do something, and Tino was determined to
fight them off.

They both had terrible secrets locked inside them like
maggots waiting to destroy any chance of happiness that
came their way.

'Don't!'

She recoiled from his cry, but the sound of it was so
distressing she reached out anyway, braving his flailing
limbs. He swore at her viciously in Greek. It was as if in
his sleeping mind the language he had been using all night
with her, the language of business and Shakespeare and
love, had been wiped from his mind by some unspeakable
wickedness from his past.

When his breathing finally steadied and he was quiet
again, she curled up, nuzzling her head into the hollow
between his shoulders, and wrapping her arms protectively
around his waist. She lay awake long into the night wondering if Stella knew... Did anyone know that Tino
Zagorakis cried out in his sleep like a wounded child?

'Lisa?'

She held her breath as he turned over, and then she
smiled in the darkness to see him returned to his normal
self.

'Why are you staring at me?' he murmured so softly she
had to lean closer to hear him. 'When you could be here—'

he turned her like lightning so that she found herself beneath him '—kissing me?'

'You were dreaming.'

'Of you,' he said confidently. Lifting himself on his arms, he stared down at her.

'No.' Lisa shook her head. 'Not me, Tino, you were dreaming about something else.'

She cried out—that small excited cry she always gave when he entered her. 'This—I must have been thinking of this,' he insisted, kissing her deeply as he started to move.

CHAPTER ELEVEN

THEY overslept on Thursday morning, waking twenty minutes before the meeting. There wasn't a moment to spare for a kiss, or a lingering touch, there were just shrieks of panic from Lisa, and an amused expression on Tino's face as he jumped out of her way when she scrambled for the shower.

'There's room enough for two,' he pointed out.

She bumped him out of the way when he tried to get in close, soaping herself vigorously. 'Oh, no, you don't—I know what two in a shower can lead to with you. Let's get this meeting over with, and the contract signed.'

'I'm all for that.' Stretching languorously, he pushed his hair back and turned his face towards the warm cascade.

'Doesn't anything unsettle you?' Lisa gazed at him.

'You, perhaps.'

But even as he spoke she remembered his nightmare, and wished there had been time to ask him about it. Leaving him in the shower, she snatched a towel from the heated rail. 'I'll see you at the meeting—don't keep me waiting.'

Lisa felt obliged to say something in answer to the look on Mike's face as she walked past him into the boardroom. Her hair was still wet, though she had gathered it on top of her head with a tortoiseshell comb, but there had been no time for make-up. 'I've been swimming, Mike.'

'Of course you have,' Mike said smoothly. 'Do I take it Zagorakis has been diving too?'

'I said swimming, Mike. In the sea.' Lisa was relieved when Tino chose that moment to walk into the room.

'I'm sorry to have kept you, gentlemen.'

No explanation required for his damp hair, or for the fact that Tino was fresh out of the shower. He had kept everyone waiting, and, from the almost imperceptible easing of muscles amongst his team, Lisa guessed for the first time ever.

The meeting lasted just over two hours, and then financial directors each made a closing statement. They had straightened out any remaining niggles between them.

'Are you ready to sign the contract?' Tino invited, looking directly at her.

Turning to her team, Lisa gazed enquiringly amongst them. There were no objections. 'Yes, we're ready.'

The deal was completed in seconds, and handshakes exchanged all round.

'If you would all like to follow me out onto the veranda,' Tino announced, 'we will raise a toast to the future in champagne.'

Lisa waited until the last taxi had pulled away before turning back to the house. Tino had suggested they have supper in the village that evening. She knew she should feel excited about that, and exultant about the deal, but his nightmare still haunted her—and so far there had been no chance to talk to him about it. She fully expected that he would refuse to discuss it, but she had to try—someone had to try to get behind his iron façade.

The village square was packed with people, but Lisa felt wonderfully safe with Tino's arm locked around her waist. He steered her towards a raised wooden stage in the centre of the square where a man had just removed the microphone from its stand. Silver haired, and with a magnificent moustache, he clearly commanded respect.

'Takis Theodopoulus,' Tino explained, whispering in Lisa's ear. He is one of the finest folk singers in Greece.

When he starts to sing he will explain everything you need to know about Greece and the Greeks.'

'But I won't understand him if he sings in Greek.'

'You'll understand Takis Theodopoulus.'

It was true, and when the folk singer began he tugged at her heartstrings in a way she'd never known before, and then Lisa noticed how captivated everyone else was—the music was like magic binding them together. Most people were holding white handkerchiefs aloft, and waving them in time to the beat, but then Tino tugged on her hand and she followed him back through the crowd.

'Now you can see why I love Stellamaris so much,' he said when they found a quieter spot. 'Life is good here—everyone expresses themselves so freely.'

When he held her glance Lisa knew they were both thinking the same thing; the past had robbed them of that freedom. 'Tino, there's something I really want to ask you about.'

'Not now.'

'Why?' Lisa dug in, prepared to be stubborn, but then she saw the hunger in his face.

'Because I can't wait any longer.'

'The flower shop?' She gazed around to make sure they were alone as he dragged her into the doorway. 'No, Tino…we can't possibly.'

'Why not? There's no one here. Everyone's in the village square listening to the singing.' Testing the door and finding it unlocked, he drew her inside.

Lisa inhaled deeply. She could grow dizzy from the scent of flowers alone, and it seemed exaggerated in the darkness… It was as if she were blindfolded and every one of her senses was enhanced…and then Tino was holding her close to him, and murmuring words in his own tongue against her neck.

'Are you warm enough?' he murmured, moving against her.

'Tino, we can't…not here. This is someone's business.'

He didn't tell her that every business on Stellamaris was his until the young owner was confident enough to run it by himself or herself. It wasn't the time, and there wasn't the time. He wanted her now with no waiting, and no explanation.

'Tino, please—I want to speak to you.'

'Not now.' He could feel her softening as he ran his fingers lightly down her spine. She had changed into one of the pretty summer dresses he had ordered for her, and she felt cool beneath his hands. She shivered beneath his touch, but not from cold. He glanced out towards the square. The light from a thousand candles told him there wasn't the slightest chance they would be disturbed… Making a sudden decision, he swung her into his arms. 'In here.' He shouldered open another door.

'I only hope you don't get splinters,' he said as he lowered her onto the wooden worktable. He spoke against her mouth, teasing her with his tongue, eager to taste her again.

'No chance of that,' Lisa murmured, feeling the cool green leaves give a little beneath her weight. And then her legs were locked around Tino's waist, and her tiny lace pants tied with ribbon had been removed.

'I made an excellent choice in underwear.'

'You made?'

'OK, so next time I'll choose them myself, and make sure they all tie like this. It's most convenient.'

'Tino… No…really, what if?'

He silenced her with a kiss, leaning into her as he loosened his belt. 'No more talking, Lisa,' he warned. 'You have to concentrate now… I haven't eaten yet, and we have a table booked at the taverna for ten o' clock.'

'You mean I'm on a fixed time slot?' She pulled back to look at him. 'I don't believe you.'

'Believe.'

He caught her to him as she cried out for him, bending his knees to achieve a better position as he sank deeply inside her. 'Is that good?'

'Oh, yes, yes, and a lot warmer too.'

'Central heating never fails.'

'Just make sure you don't stop,' Lisa warned in a whisper as her laughter was overtaken by a sob of delight.

Lifting her legs, Tino positioned them over his shoulders, supporting her back so she could lean at a more acute angle, affording him greater access.

'Good, so good,' Lisa groaned before giving herself over to a black velvet world of sensation.

Tino attended to her needs with a catalogue of perfectly judged thrusts, and when she felt the sudden tension in him Lisa anticipated the moment he would lose control. It drew an immediate response from her. Crying out excitedly, she felt the first wave of spasms hit them both at the same time like a tidal wave sweeping them to the brink of consciousness and back. And all the while, Tino held her firmly, timing his movements to extend the pleasure for her as long as he could.

'And now we eat,' he said when at last she had quietened.

'Not sure I've got enough strength left for that.'

'Are you all right?' He bent his knees to stare into her face.

'I don't know,' Lisa admitted honestly. 'I'm—'

'Exhausted? Sated? Contented?'

'All of those things.' She was exhausted, but she would never get enough of him—and as for contented? She would never be contented until she unravelled the mystery of his pain. Tenderly, as she might have touched a child, she traced the outline of his face with one hand. 'Tino, I—'

Catching hold of her hand, he silenced her, bringing it to his lips to kiss the tender palm. 'We must hurry, or we will lose our table.'

'I can't believe anyone would dare to give it away.' Lisa laughed as she hunted in the dark for her underwear.

'I receive no special treatment in Stellamaris—I should be offended if anyone tried to make a fuss of me.'

'Even me?'

'For you, I might make an exception.'

She melted into him as he dragged her close to kiss her deeply again. He smelled so good, warm, clean man, woody aftershave, and there was a fresh aroma rising from all the juicy greenery they had pounded. 'You should fasten your jeans before we leave,' she reminded him, smiling against his mouth.

'And have buttons attached to my shirt by tailor's thread in future.'

Lisa laughed as she smoothed down the creases in her own crushed dress. 'I'd only rip a hole in the fabric.'

Grabbing hold of her hand, he drew her towards the door.

She hung back. 'Tino, please…there's something I really want to ask you about.'

'Anything—but ask me later at the taverna after we've eaten. You've given me quite an appetite.'

But she couldn't ask him at the taverna—she couldn't break the mood. How could she bring up the subject of his nightmare when they were surrounded by dozens of people—most of whom he seemed to know? The brightly lit taverna was full, and the steady thrum of the bouzouki band contributed to a sensuous ambience. With all the children safely in bed with older guardians watching them, everyone was intent on wringing out the last bit of enjoyment from the night.

The tables were all draped with blue and white table-cloths that reached down almost to the floor. The tables had been set at a decent distance apart, allowing for privacy amidst the party atmosphere, and Lisa was soon as relaxed as everyone else, but she couldn't help wishing life could be less complicated.

'Why are you sighing?'

She looked up to find Tino's gaze locked onto her face. 'Because I'm so happy.'

'I'm not sure that was a happy sigh.'

'Your senses must be highly developed if you can ana-lyse a sigh over all this noise.'

'You have no idea just how highly developed they are.'

He frightened her with his perception; he excited her too...and as he continued to stare at her she found that, instead of curbing her hunger, the recent sex with him had only made her want him more.

'And now I do know what you're thinking,' he assured her, starting to stroke her leg beneath the tablecloth.

'Tino, no! You can't,' Lisa gasped, realising what he meant to do as his hand travelled steadily up her thigh. 'Not in here.'

'There's nothing I can't do,' he told her confidently. 'Just slide to the edge of your chair, and you'll find out.'

With his powerful calf wrapped around her own, he eas-ily nudged her thighs apart. Lisa could hardly believe what he was intent on doing to her. 'Tino, you really can't.' But his hand was already home, and his fingers had started working rhythmically, and persuasively.

When a sharp cry escaped her throat, he passed a napkin across the table to her with his free hand. 'I promised you an erotic adventure—bury your face in that if you don't want to draw attention to yourself.'

Peeping over the bunched-up linen square, Lisa found the apparent unconcern on Tino's face only aroused her all the more. He was staring out across the dance floor as if he were the most innocent man in the room, while she knew he was savouring every moment. But not half as much as she was, she realized, sliding to the very edge of her chair. 'You'll pay for this,' she promised him huskily.

'I certainly hope so. Now, concentrate. You're on another fixed time slot—the coffee will come round soon.'

After coffee Lisa danced with him, to slow, sensuous music that wrapped them both in a seductive cocoon. With her eyes closed she relished the feel of his strong, protective body pressing against hers.

'I think it's time to go,' Tino murmured at last, drawing her by the hand from the dance floor.

He was right, Lisa realized. They should go before their dancing caused comment. But as they were about to walk out of the taverna one of the other men caught hold of Tino's sleeve. Smiling broadly, the man rasped a few words to him in Greek.

Turning to her, Tino apologised. 'The men are about to dance the *Kalamatianos*. They have asked me to join them. It would be an insult to my friends if I refuse.'

Once again she was to be denied the chance to speak to him, Lisa realised with frustration, but, like their insatiable passion for each other, it would have to wait. She returned to her seat as Tino joined the other men on the dance floor.

The traditional dance was so powerful and so aggressively masculine Lisa started to find it unnerving. Glancing around the other women to reassure herself, she noticed how unconcerned they were—they were even urging on their men. But the more she watched and tried to tell herself that it was only a dance, the more the men's powerful response to the rhythm made it seem like a mating call, primal and fierce, that called for submission, and promised domination. The expression in the eyes of some of the men reminded her of men in the commune, and she shuddered as the intensity soared.

She couldn't take any more... She didn't even know that the music had stopped. As the cheering began Lisa blundered out of her seat, heading for the exit, blindly stumbling into tables and knocking her legs against the wooden struts.

'Lisa.'

She should have known Tino would come after her. He caught up with her before she reached the street. 'Let go of me!' She tried to pull away, but he was too strong for her.

'Lisa—what's wrong?' He held her close.

'Let me go, Tino.'

'You're shaking.'

'No, I'm not, I'm fine.'

'Then why are you running out on me?' Steering her outside, he pinned her against the wall, arms stiffly planted either side of her face. 'Tell me what's wrong, Lisa.' He gazed intently at her. 'Look at me.' He thumped the wall in frustration.

'Why? So you can frighten me with this?' She stared at one clenched fist pressed into the wall at the side of her face.

'*What?*' His face paled. 'Is that what you think of me? Is that what you think I'm trying to do to you, Lisa? No.' He turned away.

This was supposed to be about him! Lisa raged at herself inwardly. Tonight was supposed to be about Tino—not about her. What had she done? Fear made her weak...fear that, having lost control with a man for the first time in her life, she was being used for sex as her mother had been used. She would never shake it off, and Tino needed someone whole, someone untouched by shadows, someone who could help him as she never could.

'You're right,' Tino exclaimed before Lisa had chance to express her thoughts. 'I'm no good at this—I should take you back.' He held out his hand, and then, as if remembering how things were between them, he let it drop down to his side again.

By the time the first fingers of dawn were edging over her balcony Lisa had finished packing. First thing on Monday she would ring all the boutiques and find out how much money she owed Tino. The monotony of packing had soothed her a little and made her see that it was better this way. There hadn't been time to work through everything in the past that stood between them... How could there ever be enough time for that? The men's dance in the taverna had been the turning point when she had realised that they could never have a future together.

The rational part of her insisted that the dance had been nothing more than a celebration of the men's heritage—but when would the past rear its ugly head again? When would it destroy them both? She had to leave Stellamaris before that happened.

'Do you mind if I come in?'

Lisa's eyes widened with surprise to see Tino leaning into her room from the balcony outside. 'Be my guest.' She tried for casual, but her heart was juddering. She hadn't expected this. It would have been easier not to see him before she left. She still wanted him so badly it was like a continual ache in her heart, and for that reason alone she had to go. She couldn't hurt him; she could never hurt him, and if she stayed she knew she would.

She waited tensely, watching him view all the debris on her floor. There were shoeboxes and tissue paper scattered everywhere. 'I'll pay you for everything.'

He silenced her with a gesture. 'You wanted to say something to me last night, Lisa, and we never got the chance.'

'It doesn't matter now.' She looked away, ashamed that when she'd had her chance to ask him about his nightmares she had allowed her own fears to take precedence over his. Because she loved him she had to leave before she caused him any more harm—or herself.

'I hear you're leaving around noon?'

'Yes, that's right.'

'Then why don't we have breakfast together before you leave? There's plenty of time.'

'No.' She could see he was surprised at the force of her refusal. 'I'm really not hungry.'

'You don't need to be hungry to enjoy breakfast overlooking the sea.'

'It's too early for me.'

He frowned as he studied her. 'But you always like to see the sun rising over the ocean.'

'Generally, yes. But today—well, I think it's better if we make a clean break.'

'Do you really believe that?'

As he took a step forward she could have touched him. She was sure she could feel his body heat warming her. 'I still have some clearing up to do.'

'Can't you leave that for now?'

'I can't leave the room like this.' She looked around.

'I promised Stella you would come.'

Taking a deep breath, Lisa turned away from him to stare out across the balcony. Sunrise was playing tricks with the horizon and the sea wore a pink-tinted blanket of cloud. It was like a dream. If only it could have been a dream, how much easier that would have been for all of them. But it wasn't a dream, it was all too real, and how could she leave Stellamaris without saying goodbye to Stella? Saying a final goodbye to everything that Tino was.

She couldn't refuse, Lisa realised. Tino had put her in a position where she had to share breakfast with him. She shook her head as she turned back to him. 'You play dirty, Tino.'

'Yes, I know.'

'Will you give me a few minutes to clear this up?'

'I'll give you as long as you need.'

'Fifteen minutes? Out by the pool?' She didn't expect him to catch hold of her. She didn't expect to have his heady, familiar scent invading her senses. 'Yes?' she managed faintly. 'What is it, Tino?'

He didn't say anything, he just held her, and then, as if accepting it was all over between them, he let her go and stood back.

'I'm glad things have turned out well for you in the end, Lisa.'

She made a sound as if she were agreeing with him. His breath was warm on her skin, and she knew the sound of his voice would be locked in her mind for ever.

'I'll see you down there.' She kept her tone bright, and then she waited, not daring to move a muscle until he left the room. She didn't even know that she had bitten down on her lip to keep from calling him back until she tasted the warm, salty tang of her own blood.

CHAPTER TWELVE

IT WAS the sound of the piano that drew Lisa into the shadows of at the turn of the stairs. Sitting silently on a step, she peeped through the struts to see who was playing—though in her heart she already knew. Every pianist had their own unique sound that brought something of their personality to a composition... How could she have misjudged Tino so badly? How could she have attributed the presence of the piano to anyone else.. *someone with more heart*?

He was a great deal more proficient than he had pretended to be, quite remarkable, in fact, for a man who had only learned the instrument as an adult. But then Lisa guessed that Tino would have applied himself to learning the piano with the same single-minded determination he brought to everything else.

His sensitive touch drew an incredible array of sounds from the beautiful old instrument, but just as she found herself slipping away with the music he brought his hands down heavily on the keys. Recoiling at the discord, she wondered if he had seen her... She held her breath, but to her relief he left quickly in the direction of the door leading outside. She counted to a hundred before following, and it took all that time for the last ugly wave of jangling sound to disappear.

Stepping out into the fine morning light, Lisa thought the musical episode a perfect soundtrack for her affair with Tino. They were both passionate, sensitive people, but a jarring, angry chord always came between them. That was why there was no future for them together—neither of them knew how to break down the barricades they had brought with them from the past.

Her heart thundered when she saw him waiting for her. Just a tall black silhouette in the shadows, he was a man without feature or expression, a man she still didn't know in spite of all the intimacy they had shared. Shivering a little, she walked towards him. He came forward to greet her. He looked impossibly handsome, and totally assured.

'Will you come with me to meet Stella?'

'Of course.'

Just as it looked as if they might ease into a conversation, a man hurried towards them from the house.

Would they never have chance to hold a normal conversation? Lisa wondered as she stood to one side while Tino exchanged a few words with the man in Greek. He seemed pleased about something, she noticed as he turned to her.

'Will you excuse me, Lisa? I'm afraid something has come up.'

Something would always come up, she realised. 'That's fine by me. I'll go and meet Stella; don't worry.'

'I'll join you both later.'

She started to say something, but Tino was already striding away towards the house. He had recovered a lot faster than she had, Lisa reflected sadly, walking away.

'Lisa! What a lovely surprise!' Stella exclaimed, stepping out of the funicular cabin. Drawing Lisa into her arms, she drew back, and looked into her face. 'What's wrong?'

'Nothing.'

Stella shook her head in disagreement. 'I don't believe you. You're so tense. And where's Tino?' she added, looking around.

'He's been called away.'

'Ah.' Stella looked thoughtful. 'And what is this new note of resignation in your voice? Has all the fight gone out of you, Lisa?'

Lisa smiled a little. 'You think I should have rugby-tackled him to the ground?'

'You can't let him have all his own way.'

It was impossible to remain oblivious to the mischief in Stella's eyes. 'Next time,' Lisa promised without much conviction.

'So, there is to be a next time?' Stella's sharp gaze focused on her face.

'No, Stella, this is my last day on Stellamaris.'

Stella sighed as she linked arms with Lisa and drew her up the path. 'Don't be impatient with Tino, Lisa, he's a very busy man.'

'I'm not impatient.' Just disappointed, sad, and angry with myself for thinking it could be any different.

'I should think not,' Stella exclaimed, snapping her out of it. 'I am here.'

Lisa squeezed Stella's arm affectionately. She had to put Tino out of her mind, but Stella wasn't making it easy for her.

After breakfast Stella raised the subject of Tino again.

'I'm not disappointed,' Lisa lied. 'He invited me for breakfast, I just thought he might make the effort to turn up.'

'He's a good man, Lisa.'

Lisa turned her head away. She wasn't ready to hear that, not from Stella, not from someone she trusted as much as she trusted Stella. Then Stella covered her hand with her own as if she sensed her turmoil. 'Don't...' Lisa pulled her hand away. 'I might cry.'

'And if you do?' Stella demanded gently. 'What is wrong with crying, Lisa? Why are you so ashamed of your emotions?' Digging into her pocket, she pulled out a crisply laundered handkerchief and handed it over. 'Sometimes the view in Stellamaris is enough to make me cry...and sometimes my memories are enough. Other times I cry because I am so happy—like the time when Giorgio told me how much he loved Arianna. I'm not ashamed of how I feel. I rejoice in the gift of life in all its guises. And I am Greek,' she added, smiling mischievously, 'so naturally I feel things very deeply, as we Greeks do. We have a hunger for life, Lisa…a passion.'

'I have all those things inside me, Stella.' Lisa's voice was desperate. 'But I don't know how to set them free.'

Stella touched her arm. 'Then I must help you,' she said gently.

'No one can do that.'

'How many Greeks do you know?'

The expression on Stella's face forced a smile onto Lisa's lips. 'Too few, and one too many.'

'Tino?' Stella asked shrewdly. 'He's the one too many?'

'Yes,' Lisa admitted, 'though I don't really know him.'

'What do you want to know about him? Shall I tell you that he is the most wonderful man I have ever known? No? Why are you shaking your head at me, Lisa? Do you find that so hard to believe? Let me tell you a little more about Tino. He paid for Arianna to go to the music conservatoire. Without him my daughter's wonderful voice would never have been recognised. And he gave me more than I could ever tell you… Far more than money, Tino is the son I never had. The apartment block where I live when I am in Athens, and the cottage here in Stellamaris—Constantine gave them to me. He gave me the whole block of apartments, Lisa.' Stella touched her hand to her chest to express her emotion. 'And still you frown?' She shook her head.

'I just can't believe we're talking about the same man. You told me once you'd known Tino *for ever*, so you must have known his family. Can't you tell me a little about them so that I can understand him better?'

It was hard to believe how rapidly Stella's expression changed from open and friendly to completely shut.

'Tino hasn't told you about his background?'

'About his family, no.'

'Then I can't tell you either. I'm sorry, Lisa, only Tino can tell you about his past.'

And he would never do that, Lisa realised.

'I'm very sorry to have deserted you, ladies.'

'Tino.' Lisa's heart turned over as she gazed at him. 'I wasn't sure I would see you again.'

He made a casual gesture. 'They wanted me to check on something inside the house—'

'We ate breakfast without you,' Stella cut in. 'We didn't know how long you would be, Constantine.'

'And I apologise, *Ya-ya*, for not being there to greet you this morning.' Embracing Stella, Tino kissed her affectionately on both cheeks.

'Whatever took you away,' Stella said, 'I can see it was important from your face, so I will forgive you, Constantine.'

'It was important, *Ya-ya*. It was of the utmost importance.'

Lisa's stomach clenched. Why was he looking at her? 'You haven't been having second thoughts about the contract, have you?'

Tipping his head to one side, Tino smiled at her. 'I do think of some things other than business, you know.'

'But not often enough,' Stella observed tartly. 'And now, if you two will excuse me, I should like to take a walk around the gardens to be sure that your flowers are at their best for our festival tonight, Constantine.'

'Of course.' Lisa turned to her. 'The taxi driver told me that you fill your houses with flowers for May Day here on Stellamaris.'

'Not until later today,' Stella explained. 'After our siesta this afternoon there will be a procession through the village, and then when all the houses are decorated there will be a party in the village square.'

'Another party.' Lisa smiled.

'Life can be hard.' Stella shrugged. 'So we Greeks celebrate whenever we can—' Reaching out, she rested her hand on Lisa's arm. 'You must make time to be happy too, Lisa.'

'Will I see you before I go?' Lisa's throat tightened.

'I'm sure we will see each other.'

When Stella smiled at her, Lisa wanted to go and throw her arms around the elderly Greek woman and beg her not to leave. It didn't make any sense, Lisa reasoned, watching Stella make her way down the path. She had stood on her own two feet since she could stand, she ran a huge and complex business, she had money and prestige, but right now all she wanted was for Stella to be her friend so she could learn all the things she didn't know or understand— all the important things, the things she had never found time for in the past.

'I'm told your suitcase is still upstairs.'

Lisa came to with a jolt. Tino couldn't have made it any plainer that he couldn't wait for her to leave. 'I'm sorry, Tino, I forgot the case. I did mean to bring it down.'

'Don't worry, I'll do that for you. Just show me where it is. Are you thinking about business again?' he said when she didn't reply.

'Actually, I was thinking about changing my life.'

'Changing your life? That's rather momentous, isn't it?'

'Yes, it is. But Stella Panayotakis talks a lot of sense... She's made me think; she's made me re-evaluate everything. Is Stella a relative of yours, Tino?'

'As good as.'

'Only *Ya-ya* means—'

'Grandma. Yes, I know, Lisa. About these changes...'

He held the door into the house for her. 'Tell me something about them.'

'I would never relinquish my seat on the board at Bond Steel,' Lisa began slowly, thinking aloud, 'but I have many talented people on my team and with this cash injection they will hardly need me on a daily basis. The job isn't enough for me any more.' She shrugged and flashed a wry smile at him. 'Before you ask, I don't know what I *do* want to do yet. Let's just say Stellamaris has made me greedy— and don't look so worried,' she added dryly. 'What I want, we both know you can't give me.'

'And what's that?' Tino asked as he followed her into the house.

'I want stability, a broader view on life, a long-term future to look forward to…and I don't ever want to stop working.'

'I'm very pleased to hear it.'

'I just want to make room in my life for other things.' How strange it felt to be walking up the stairs with Tino discussing her future like this as if they were two strangers whose paths had briefly crossed.

'Here we are,' he said, opening the door to her suite. 'Just show me where the suitcase is, and I'll take it down for you.'

Lisa stood transfixed on the threshold of the room. Then, walking past him, she turned full circle. 'What are these?'

'Flowers,' Tino said dryly. 'Remember? You said that flowers would be special. Don't you like them?'

'I don't know what to say.' Every surface in the room was covered in the most beautiful floral arrangements Lisa had ever seen. She wanted to believe they were for her, but she knew they couldn't be. And then she remembered. 'Of course, it's May Day.' She turned, and gave Tino a quick smile, remembering that this scene would be reproduced in every household on the island. For a moment she had imagined—Lisa shuddered, realising how close she had come to making the most terrible fool of herself. 'I'm sorry, Tino. I shouldn't be keeping you waiting like this. My suitcase is over there behind that chair.' She saw the shadow flit across his face. In these days of equality, of course, she shouldn't expect him to carry it for her. She should take it down herself. 'The flowers are really beautiful,' she said, when he didn't move. 'You have some wonderful traditions on the island.'

'Yes, we do.'

His voice was expressionless, and then she noticed that his eyes were the only part of him that did show emotion—and the look in them frightened her.

As the moment stretched on Lisa knew that she was only making things worse with her indecisiveness. What on earth was she waiting for, anyway? 'I expect my taxi will have arrived by now.' Walking past Tino, she grabbed hold of the suitcase and started for the door. Her foot had barely touched the landing when he yanked her back inside the room again.

'What do you think you are doing?' Lisa stared angrily at his hand on her arm. 'What's wrong with you, Tino?'

'What's wrong with *me*?' He slammed the door. 'This is the matter.' His furious stare embraced the room.

'The flowers?' Lisa said uncertainly, putting down her case.

'Yes! The flowers! What the hell else could I be referring to?'

'I've already said how nice they are—'

'Nice?' He looked away as if he needed time to compose himself, and then, staring towards the heavens, he cursed in Greek.

The fact that she had made a terrible mistake didn't come to Lisa like a thunderbolt, it was a long-drawn-out torture that dripped ice through her veins until finally it reached her heart: *the flowers were for her*... Of course they were for her! She had schooled herself always to think the worst of people. Any normal woman would have seen that immediately, the moment Tino had opened the door—the moment she'd stepped over the threshold, the moment she'd seen what he had done for her. 'Tino.' Lisa found that her throat had dried to the point where she could hardly make herself heard. 'I'm so sorry, I didn't realise...and they're so beautiful.'

'I thought this was what you wanted.' He stopped and passed a hand over his eyes as if he wanted to blot out the moment when he had decided to lay his heart at her feet so she could trample on it.

'I'm so ashamed... I thought—'

He whirled around to confront her. 'You should be ashamed. You're just like all the rest. You tell me that you don't want jewels—that flowers are what touch you the most...but when I give you flowers you are disappointed and you treat my gift with contempt.'

'Tino, please—listen to me.' Taking hold of his arm, Lisa flinched as he pulled away.

'We'd better not keep your taxi waiting.' He didn't look at her. 'If your pilot misses his slot you won't be able to leave the island tonight.'

Lisa braced herself as the jet took off, soaring high above the clouds over Stellamaris.

On the journey to the airport she had seen the flower-laden carts with children sitting on the buckboards tossing handfuls of blooms to crowds lining the streets. The car had been forced to slow, so she hadn't missed a single detail of the procession. Everyone had been in such high spirits and she had longed to be part of it...with Tino.

To make matters worse, when she'd said goodbye to Maria before leaving the villa she had learned that Tino had been up before anyone else that morning choosing flowers for her in the garden. He had carried the arrangements up to her room while she was having breakfast with Stella, not trusting anyone else to do it; that was the important matter that had delayed him.

It was as well she was leaving. She damaged everyone she cared about. Her mother had sacrificed everything for her, and Jack Bond—a man she still found it hard to call her father—had looked for a love she could never give him. She could see it all now with agonising clarity, and knew she couldn't risk causing any more harm. She cared too much for Tino to stay.. and, even had she wanted to stay, he had made it very clear that he didn't want her in his life. Business was her forte. She was good at that. She had done the deal she had set out to do. She had to be satisfied. She had to accept there were some things in life she would never master, and love was just one of them.

Seated in his study, Tino grimaced. The suspicion that he had been tricked was only boosted by the sound of Lisa's jet passing overhead.

Emotions had no part to play in business and he had made a fundamental error allowing her in. He only had to think of the flowers to know she had made a fool of him… Had she used him for sex? Or had she used sex to secure the deal? Either way this wasn't over. He couldn't just let her walk away…

This time he didn't ring the bell and wait patiently for her housekeeper to answer it, he thundered on her door with his fist, and then shouted her name through the letterbox.

'All right, all—' Lisa pressed back against the wall as Tino stalked past her. 'Nice to see you too,' she added under her breath as she followed him into her den. 'Would you like a drink?' She glanced down at her own flute of champagne, feeling the world had gone mad, or that she had fallen asleep and had to be dreaming.

'Celebrating, Lisa?'

The tone of Tino's voice soon brought her round. She had never seen him like this before. 'Could you snarl a little louder? I didn't quite hear you.'

'I said, are you celebrating, Lisa?'

It was Vera's night off, and Tino's visit seemed so unreal. It was hard to believe how much he affected her. She had to keep staring at him just to make sure she wasn't dreaming. She felt exhilarated briefly, but then caution took over, and now the expression on his face hardly invited enthusiasm. Maybe she would do better to feel intimidated...but instead of that she felt sad—sad for both of them. They were both so enmeshed in the past, so emotionally scarred, they didn't know how to express themselves other than through business. They both had so much, but where things that really mattered were concerned they had nothing.

The only way forward was to keep everything on an impersonal level, Lisa decided, as if they were in a business meeting. But first she had some apologising to do. 'I'm glad you've come.' She held open the door of her den for him. 'I've been hoping for an opportunity to say how sorry I am about the flowers.'

'The flowers?'

As Tino frowned Lisa realised her mistake. He couldn't have cared less about the flowers. He had something a lot more important on his mind—his pride, perhaps? And then she realised that she was still holding the glass of champagne in her hand, and that he was staring at it. She felt bound to explain. 'I was just drinking a toast to my new life.'

'Your new life?' He cut across her. His eyes narrowed

with suspicion. 'The last time we spoke you mentioned changes. You move fast.'

His tone was hostile, but one of them had to keep calm. 'So many questions, Tino,' she said lightly. 'Why don't you join me in a glass of champagne?'

Instead of answering, he stood vibrating with some inner conflict.

'So, why are you here?' she prompted, wanting him to say something, anything.

He shook his head, his face a rigid mask. 'You've got a nerve.'

Lisa stiffened defensively. 'What are you talking about?'

'Do you really think you can use me?'

'Use you?' All Lisa's thoughts on staying calm evaporated. 'And just how am I supposed to have used you?'

'I think you know. What was I to you, Lisa—some sort of device to excise your ghosts?'

'*My* ghosts?' She stared at him.

He stared back at her unflinching.

'Or is there something else? Don't tell me—' she held up her hand '—I forgot to sign something.' She stared accusingly at his jacket pocket. 'Well? What are you waiting for? We might as well get this over with.'

His expression turned glacial. 'Is that what you think of me?'

'I think I understand you pretty well, yes.'

'Understand me? You understand nothing about me.'

He couldn't believe this was happening. He couldn't believe she could arouse such feeling in him. They were eyeing each other like gladiators in the coliseum. There was so much passion in the room he could feel it swirling around them.

It was the last thing he had wanted, the last thing he had anticipated; emotion was his *bête noire*, something he avoided at all cost because he didn't understand it. He didn't have a strategy to deal with it. And he didn't want to understand it—something so unpredictable, so unquantifiable?

He turned away feeling frustration building inside him again. He couldn't find the words to express his feelings—and all he could be sure about was that coming to see Lisa was the worst mistake he had ever made.

'I don't know why you came here,' she threw at him.

How could he tell her when he hardly knew himself?

'I think it's better if you go now and never come back.'

Did she have someone else? The thought speared through him as she spoke. 'Is there someone else?' *Was this jealousy?*

'What?' She stared at him incredulously.

'Don't hold back on my account, Lisa. If you've got someone else here in England, just tell me.' His voice sounded hoarse. The cost of exposing his innermost thoughts to her was terrible—far worse than he had expected.

'Someone else?' As they stared at each other Lisa saw the expression in Tino's eyes change. This was not the formidable business opponent she knew, or even the confident man. Those eyes were the eyes of the child who had been locked in a nightmare, the child who had cried out to her in the night. For just those few seconds it was as if all the barricades Tino had raised against the world and against her had disappeared, but he built them up again so fast, she was left wondering if she had imagined it.

He was just as damaged on the inside as she was. He would always wonder if he was capable of feeling anything beyond some fleeting triumph in business. She could only hope he wasn't destined to remain as numb in his heart as she was. 'There's no one else, Tino,' she said quietly. 'There never can be anyone.'

'So, your life will always be empty.'

'It's better that way. It would be irresponsible of me to involve anyone in my life, when I have nothing to offer them.'

'You're wrong, Lisa.' Tino spoke from the heart as images of Stella and Arianna, as well as many others, crowded his mind. 'You have had an empty life, I understand that. But it can get better, I promise you.'

'You promise me, Tino? What do you promise me? That in time I can learn to care as much as you do?'

She used sarcasm like a shield, and he deserved her cynicism. 'I admit that I've still got a long way to go, but at least I have started the journey—' He stopped, self-conscious at showing such candour on a subject he was still building up faith in himself. 'And it's not that bad.'

Was this feeling currently tearing her apart Tino's idea of 'not that bad'? Lisa wondered, drawing a steadying breath. 'Then, all I can say is, you're very lucky, Tino…but I know that letting people in can never be for me.'

'But you were drinking a toast to your new life.'

'New pastimes, new occupations to run alongside Bond Steel, not a whole raft of personal involvements I know can only end in disaster.'

'A whole raft?'

For a moment she thought he was trying not to smile—and not in a nasty way, or a point-scoring way. 'You know what I mean.' She sounded edgy, and she was. She was determined he wouldn't turn this back into some sort of emotional ping-pong. She was going to stick to the facts whatever he threw at her.

'So, tell me about these changes.'

'I'm not even sure about them myself yet.' She couldn't see a hint of a smile on his face now, and was reassured enough to ask, 'Would you like that drink now?'

'Before I go?'

He was gently teasing her, Lisa realised, careful to remain unmoved. 'Yes. Champagne all right for you?' She glanced at the shelf where all her crystal glasses were lined up in rows.

'Lalique?' Tino murmured, but, in case she thought he was impressed, he added wryly, 'Are they dusty?'

'I doubt it.' Lisa smiled a little too now, but she still wasn't quite sure she was ready for his humour. 'Vera looks after me too well for anything in here to be dusty.' She knew what he was getting at. They both had so much, so many material things, but they had no one special to share any of it with.

'So, come on,' he pressed, 'I'm waiting to hear about these changes to your life—'

'Like I said, I'm not sure, Tino.'

'I think we'd better drink a general toast,' he suggested dryly.

Pouring the champagne, Lisa was careful not to touch his hand when she gave him the glass.'

'To us,' he said.

'To us,' Lisa echoed, staring at him over the rim of her glass. 'Won't you sit down?'

She pointed to the sofa where he assumed she had been making herself comfortable when he'd arrived. There was a cosy throw to wrap around her pyjamas flung over the back of it, and a pair of ridiculous fluffy slippers sticking out underneath. And now he saw that her feet were bare, and that her toenails looked like perfect pink shells...

Putting his glass down on the table, he looked at her... He could see she wanted to say something. 'Lisa?' he prompted. 'What is it?'

'About the flowers—'

When he had first arrived at the apartment, and she had tried to apologise, he had been ungracious. His head had been filled with memories of the hurt and anger he had felt when she'd walked into her room at Villa Aphrodite and made a mockery of his gift. But now it was different, now they were both calmer…and the least he owed her was a chance to explain. He held her gaze, willing her to go on.

'The flowers *were* special, Tino, very special, and so was the thought behind them. I can't believe I didn't realise they were your gift to me.'

The way she was looking at him now, with her eyes so wide and troubled, touched something deep inside him, and feelings welled up from some hidden place so that he wanted to go to her and hold her in his arms.

'I couldn't believe you would do something like that for me, that anyone would.'

She made a helpless gesture, as if she was hunting for the right words with the same lack of success he had run up against when he had first arrived. 'Won't you sit down with me?' he suggested gently.

She came to then, and stared at him with sharper focus. 'No—I'd better not. And, Tino, that toast we made—' She frowned as she looked at her glass. 'When I said, "to us", of course I meant "to us" independently.'

'Of course.' He kept his expression neutral. 'Us. Independently,' he added dryly.

This awkwardness between them was new. They could rage at each other, or deal analytically with each other across a boardroom table quite comfortably, but this tip-toeing around each other was like starting over, working through something very carefully to find out if it could be safe…

'I can't bear to be hurt, Tino.'

The frank confession made him doubly alert. She was looking at him, totally oblivious to the fact that she had her arms wrapped around her waist in a defensive gesture.

'I have to protect myself.'

'From me?'

She looked away.

'Lisa, please believe me… I do know what you're trying to say. Trust doesn't come in a rush, it grows slowly with time…and that's the same for everyone, not just you and me.'

She flinched at that. 'There is no you and me, Tino. There never can be. We're no good for each other. Surely you must know that. You need someone strong.'

'How do you know what I need?'

'I heard you cry out in the night, Tino. I may not know much about you, but that night proved to me that you're not the product of an ordinary childhood.'

'An ordinary childhood?' he repeated her words softly. 'Whatever that might be.'

'I don't pretend to know what happened to you, Tino. I only know what I see in front of me now, and what I heard that night when you cried out in terror like a little boy who was very frightened.'

He looked at her searchingly. 'No one has ever told me I do that before.'

'Maybe you've never done it before.'

'Maybe I've never felt safe enough to do it before.' He stopped. He'd gone too far and automatically pulled back. 'Truce?' Now it was his turn to feel awkward.

'Truce,' Lisa agreed softly, 'Don't worry,' she whispered, as if that was all he had on his mind, 'I won't tell anyone.'

'I never thought that you would.'

He reached out, and then stopped himself, clenching his hands to prevent himself from weakening. After another period of silence had elapsed and the tension between them had subsided, he tried again. 'You say we're no good for each other? I think you're wrong.'

'You would think that, but then you always believe you're right.'

He was relieved to see that as she made the comment it almost brought a smile to her lips.

Neither of them moved for a while, but then she surprised him, coming to sit down as he had hoped she would on the sofa at his side. For a moment he thought she had opened her heart to the possibility that there was another way than to live without love, but he was soon disillusioned. She had only come close to him to drive her point home...

Clenching both her fists, she pressed them into her chest so hard her knuckles turned white. 'There's nothing in here, Tino.'

He couldn't bear to see the look on her face. 'No!' Was that voice his? Without thinking, he dragged her to him.

'Please, Tino, let me go... I have nothing inside me... I've got nothing to give you.'

'No, Lisa, you're wrong. I can see inside you, and you're beautiful.'

And when she searched his face, and he saw the doubt fighting with her need to believe him, he shook his head and smiled tenderly at her. 'Don't you see, Lisa? We're the saving of each other...' And then he held her as if he would never let her go until she finally relaxed, and began to shudder uncontrollably in his arms.

'Do you really think so?'

Her voice was tiny like a child's and it made him want to cry for the first time he could remember...for both of them. 'I know it.'

Still sensing her doubt, he cupped her chin and brought her to face him again. 'I know it's true, because I love you, Lisa. I love you so much you've got no idea.' He kissed her then, and it was a beginning... It was as if they had never kissed before; it was a revelation to them both, like coming home.

CHAPTER THIRTEEN

LISA was still warm from the bath. How could he have forgotten how wonderful she felt in his arms when the need rose in them both like a white-hot flame?

'It was good, wasn't it?' she whispered when he finally stopped kissing her.

'*Is* good,' Tino corrected, still holding her, staring into her eyes. 'Better than good.'

How could she hold back her feelings when she didn't want to? How could she hold firm when her body, her heart, her mind, her soul called out to him, and when she only felt complete when she was with him? 'I love you, Tino.'

'Are you asking me, or telling me?'

They both laughed, and she buried her face against his chest. 'Do I still sound so uncertain?' She watched his lips tug up in a half-smile, 'I…love…you.'

He swept her up into his arms and carried her to the bedroom to seal the pledge they had made to each other. Lowering her down onto the bed, he dropped the towel he had been wearing round his waist, and slipped beneath the covers, drawing her into his arms. Stroking her hair, he dropped kisses on her eyes, on her cheek, on her brow…

'This is good,' he said tenderly. 'The best thing in the world is being in bed with you.'

'It's so much softer than a table,' she teased him. 'The worktable in a florist's shop,' she reminded him, 'the board-room table.'

'Yours, or mine?'

'Both, if I have my way.'

'Then it's to be hoped you do—I'm keen to make sure our lovemaking never becomes predictable.'

'No chance of that—' Lisa gasped as Tino moved down the bed, kissing every inch of her on the way. He flung back the covers so that the subdued light from the bedside lamp played across her naked body, turning it a deeper shade of peach.

'You're so beautiful,' he murmured, tracing the contours of her breasts and belly with the lightest touch to bring her pleasure. 'I want to taste you.'

Throwing her head back on the soft bank of pillows, Lisa moaned softly as he moved between her thighs, pressing her legs back with his warm palms until she was completely open for him, completely ready... She could refuse him nothing...not even her heart.

His dark hair was so glossy in the lamplight, so silky to her touch as she laced her fingers through the thick waves to urge him on... His tongue was every bit as skilful as his fingers, and there was no part of her he did not understand, or know how to play for the greatest pleasure. But as her excitement grew to fever pitch he drew back, smiling down at her, his eyes dark with passion, and his smile wolfish in the half-light.

'Don't keep me waiting—'

'Or?' he demanded.

'If you're naughty, I shall have to punish you.'

Arousal hit them at the same moment, and as their eyes locked Tino knew they were thinking the same thing. They had both suffered the consequences of violence, but they had worked through their fears together, and it had brought them closer than either of them had anticipated. They could push the boundaries because they loved each other, and because they could trust each other completely, and because, at last, they both knew without any doubt at all that they were safe.

'Better?' he asked Lisa later when she lay quiet in his arms.

'Can't speak...no strength.' Her body was floating on another dimension. She couldn't have called it back even had she wanted to.

'All the shadows gone?'

'Shadows?'

'We both have them,' Tino told her, shifting his head on the pillows to meet her gaze. 'You can't hide from someone who has spent his whole life blanking out the past—'

'That works both ways, Tino.'

'I know about the commune,' he said. 'I know about all the terrible things you saw while you were living there. I understand your reasons for running away, and for going back to live with your father. You were right to do that, Lisa. And in the end your mother did her best for you. No child should have been exposed to the dangers you were exposed to, and I believe she helped you to get out of there just in time.'

'Who told you all this?'

'Does it matter?'

It had to be Mike, Lisa realised. She hadn't confided the truth about her mother's extreme lifestyle to another living soul.

'Don't be angry with Mike,' Tino said as he read her mind. 'He only has your best interests at heart.'

'I'm not angry. It's just that I never talk about the past in case anyone thinks I'm looking for sympathy, or help. I know that no one can help me. I can only help myself.'

'If you thought of it as understanding, rather than sympathy, you might find other people out there just like you. You can share the road back with someone else, Lisa, someone who is also trying to break free from the past.'

'With you, Tino?'

'Why not? Just because your mother's life was chaotic

doesn't mean you have to order your own life with such an unforgiving hand.'

'I'm getting better.' She viewed their sated forms with a wry glance.

'You are better, because you know you can trust me, and you know that violence will never have any part to play in our relationship. Why shouldn't lovemaking be fun? Who's to say what's right or wrong between consenting adults, as long as no one else is hurt by their actions? What happens between us in the bedroom stays between us. And if you don't like something, you only have to tell me.'

'I like everything,' Lisa assured him, snuggling close, already feeling her body starting to yearn for his attention.

'Not yet,' Tino whispered, soothing her with long strokes down her back. 'First we talk.'

'First you talk.' Lisa raised herself on one arm to stare at him. 'You know so much about me, and I need to understand your nightmares. Tell me about the past, Tino.'

'I don't want to burden you.'

Putting one finger over his lips, she shook her head, silently encouraging him, prepared to wait for however long it took.

'Stella Panayotakis took care of me when I was a boy,' he said at last.

'Didn't your mother take care of you?'

'I never knew my mother—she didn't want anything to do with me.'

'Tino, I'm so sorry... I had no idea.'

'No one does. That's the joke. Tino Zagorakis, the Greek tycoon, doesn't even know if he is a Greek.'

'But your name?'

'I took it from the van that came to the orphanage each week.. "Zagorakis Cleaning Services". What a joke, eh?'

'The orphanage? Oh, Tino.' This was no joke, and Lisa fell silent the moment he started speaking again.

'Everything inside the orphanage was grey until the day that Stella Panayotakis came to work there. Stella taught me that life could be bigger than my life in the orphanage. She said my life could be exciting. She told me about the world outside the orphanage—a world that was raw, and vivid, and only waiting for me to take my part in it. She put dreams into my head, and promised they would all come true if only I believed... It was hard, Lisa, really hard and Stella Panayotakis made me believe.'

'And when you were successful you gave her an apartment building.'

'She told you that?'

'Stella is your greatest fan.'

'And now, I have more plans, bigger plans.'

Tino's enthusiasm was infectious. 'What are your plans, Tino? Please tell me about them.'

'Well...I am going to have more places like Stellamaris.'

'More islands?' Lisa drew up in amazement.

'I'm sorry, *pethi mou*, you do not know.'

'I don't know what?'

'When I bought Stellamaris, I named it for Stella, and then I used it as my base.'

'Your base? You mean for your business?'

'For my other business.'

'Stop talking in riddles,' Lisa warned, dropping a kiss on his chest.

'I bring young people to Stellamaris, and some older people too...to find themselves. The island is a sanctuary, a place to start again, and for some, a place to start. Many of the people on Stellamaris began their lives in orphanages. I make sure there is training there for everyone, and that Stella visits frequently. Stella was my inspiration, and now she is theirs.'

'Now I understand why you're so close to Arianna.'

'Stella was a single mother, and it was very hard for her

back then. Don't look so impressed, Lisa. I don't deserve any praise. I did nothing special…it was all Stella's doing. All I have ever done is give people the tools to help themselves. Their achievements are all their own.'

'And now?' Lisa looked at him intently. 'Tell me about your new plans?'

'They're not so much new, as an extension of my existing scheme. I have accumulated massive wealth, and now I want to use that money to help others as Stella helped me. I want to extend my programme right across Greece to begin with.'

'Nothing too ambitious, then,' Lisa teased him gently.

'Very ambitious,' Tino admitted, 'and because of that I will need someone at my side. I can't even start the work I want to do until I find that one special person—someone who shares my aims, my desires, my dreams…someone who knows what it feels like to be on the outside looking in. Can you be that person, Lisa?'

'Are you offering me a job?'

Tino tilted his head as he pretended to consider this. 'Can you think of anyone better qualified to take on this task than a successful businesswoman who has accepted that she can delegate some of her duties to other members of her team at Bond Steel, a woman who has suddenly discovered she has a heart, a woman who knows what it is to be an outcast, a woman of principle, a woman who is every bit as driven as I am, a woman who has recently declared she is looking for radical change in her life?'

Closing her eyes, Lisa took time over framing her answer. 'All this—' she touched his face gently in wonder '—and a new job in just one working week.'

'Exactly as we planned,' Tino pointed out. 'We make a great team.'

'And if I was looking for something more?'

'Something more?'

'More than just a job, more than simply joining your organisation to help you with this new project?' She tensed as Tino stretched beyond her to reach for his clothes. 'What are you doing?'

'Looking for something…'

Seeing the velvet case, Lisa exclaimed with concern. 'You were supposed to take those back.'

'Surely you didn't expect me to take them back to the shop after you'd worn them, did you?'

Remembering where she'd worn them, Lisa blushed. 'Perhaps not.'

'Oh, look, here's another one.' Falling back onto the pillows, Tino dragged her down with him. Now there were two velvet boxes. 'Which one? You choose.'

'You shouldn't be buying me presents.'

'Buying gifts for you is one impulse I will never allow you to control,' he informed her. 'Now, which one do you choose?'

'They say all the best things come in small packages.'

'Not always.'

'But maybe you are right this time,' Tino conceded. 'Why don't you open the small box and find out?'

Taking it from him, Lisa pressed the small gilt catch and gasped as the lid flew open. The emerald ring was a perfect match to the fabulous earrings. 'What's this? A down payment on my first month's wages?'

'You wish.'

'So, what am I to think?' she demanded wryly.

Taking her left hand, he tested the ring for size on her marriage finger. 'Thank goodness, it fits perfectly. Oh, and there's one more thing.'

'Yes?' Lisa could hardly tear her gaze away from the incredible jewel on her finger.

'When we're in bed,' Tino continued sternly, 'there'll be

no more talk of wages and business. In our private life there will be just you, me, and our love under discussion.'

'Our love…'

'We can hardly be married without it.'

'Married?'

'Is this going to be another one of your business contracts?' he teased.

'Not just another contract,' Lisa argued firmly. 'The most important contract of all.'

'So, will you shake on the deal?' He started to smile.

'I'll certainly show some reaction,' she promised huskily when he drew her close to kiss her again.

EPILOGUE

'NO, NO, no…' Sprawled on the floor with her legs stuck out in front of her, Lisa waggled her finger.

'That won't work… You have to do it like this,' Tino informed her, sweeping their son onto his shoulders.

Now, instead of screaming with frustration, the determined two-year-old was screaming with laughter as Tino galloped with him around the room.

'Come on, let's gather up the pieces of your jigsaw,' Lisa suggested to the fairy princess at her side. Elena took her puzzles seriously, and hadn't welcomed her brother's interference, but the fact that she had insisted on wearing a tinsel headband and a pair of wings while she worked made Lisa think that Elena would grow up to have just the right mix of intellect and playfulness.

And who would have imagined that Tino would turn into such a wonderful family man? Lisa mused, pausing to watch him for a moment…or that she would have a wardrobe full of musty suits, and paint-spattered jeans?

And wasn't this better? Wasn't this wonderful? And wasn't the sight of their newest taverna going up to provide training for a whole new group of youngsters the most thrilling deal either of them had ever pulled off?

'You're looking very thoughtful,' Tino observed, hunkering down beside her. It took some skill to keep Lucas balanced on his shoulders when the toddler was intent on hanging upside down.

'I'm just blessing the fact that our paths crossed at all,' Lisa admitted wryly. 'That was some quirk of fate.'

'Quirk of fate?' Tino stared at her. 'Our meeting was no accident, Lisa…'

'What do you mean?'

Lowering his son to the ground as Elena held out her hand to Lucas to take him out to play, Tino explained, 'I read about you, then I saw your photograph…and the rest is history.'

'I suppose you were determined to bring me to heel? You were,' she accused him fondly. 'I can see it written all over your face…'

'Maybe,' Tino confessed, slanting her a smile.

That was the point…the whole point. They were so similar they could read each other like a book. But it had been more than the challenge that had brought him to the offices of Bond Steel that day… When he had first heard Lisa's story, something deep inside him had cried out to meet her. With a history such as they shared you needed more than one lifetime to try and explain yourself. With Lisa, he never had to try; she just knew.

He had always wondered, feared, that the past might have left some indelible scar on him, but, although from the earliest days Lisa had tested his control to the limits and beyond, she had helped him prove that he had left the past behind, and that none of the violence had travelled with him.

He only felt complete when she was with him, and now they had children too…a family, the one thing he had always dreamed about when he was a child in the orphanage. And even now, gazing at Lisa, and Elena, and Lucas, he could hardly believe the joy they gave him. The love of a woman was a wonderful thing, but the love of a family was the greatest gift of all.

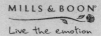

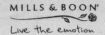

FREE!

4 Books
and a surprise gift!

We would like to take this opportunity to thank you for reading this Mills & Boon® book by offering you the chance to take FOUR more specially selected titles from the Modern Romance™ series absolutely FREE! We're also making this offer to introduce you to the benefits of the Reader Service™—

- ★ **FREE home delivery**
- ★ **FREE gifts and competitions**
- ★ **FREE monthly Newsletter**
- ★ **Exclusive Reader Service offers**
- ★ **Books available before they're in the shops**

Accepting these FREE books and gift places you under no obligation to buy, you may cancel at any time, even after receiving your free shipment. Simply complete your details below and return the entire page to the address below. You don't even need a stamp!

YES! Please send me 4 free Modern Romance books and a surprise gift. I understand that unless you hear from me. I will receive 6 superb new titles every month for just £2.75 each, postage and packing free. I am under no obligation to purchase any books and may cancel my subscription at any time. The free books and gift will be mine to keep in any case.

P5ZEF

Ms/Mrs/Miss/Mr ....Initials........................

BLOCK CAPITALS PLEASE

Surname ....

Address...

....

....Postcode ....

Send this whole page to:
UK: FREEPOST CN81, Croydon, CR9 3WZ